Why Men Are Afraid of Women

Winner of

Why Men Are Afraid of Women

Stories by François Camoin

The University of Georgia Press
Athens

© 1984 by François Camoin
Published by the University of Georgia Press
Athens, Georgia 30602
All rights reserved

Set in Linotron 202 Baskerville
The paper in this book meets the guidelines for
permanence and durability of the Committee on
Production Guidelines for Book Longevity of the
Council on Library Resources.

Printed in the United States of America
88 87 86 85   5 4 3 2

Library of Congress Cataloging in Publication Data

Camoin, François Andre, 1939–
    Why men are afraid of women.

    (The Flannery O'Connor award for short fiction)
    Contents: Miami—It could happen—Peacock
blue—[etc.]
    I. Title.   II. Series.
PS3553.A437W48   1984   813'.54   84-1374
ISBN 0-8203-0722-x (alk. paper)

Acknowledgments

The author and the publisher gratefully acknowledge the magazines in which stories in this volume first appeared.

The Black Warrior Review: "Cheerful Wisdom"
The Georgia Review: "It Could Happen"
Mid-American Review: "La Vida"
Mississippi Review: "Miami"
Missouri Review: "A Hunk of Burning Love"
Nimrod: "Sometimes the Wrong Thing Is the Right Thing"
Quarterly West: "The Amelia Barons"
Utah Holiday: "Peacock Blue"
Vanderbilt Review (Texas): "Home Is the Blue Moon Cafe"
Western Humanities Review: "Diehl: The Wandering Years" and "A Special Case"

For my sisters

DANIÈLE DOCTOROW

SUZANNE DOCTOROW MCDOUGALL

Contents

Miami

My wife Marge is lying on the bed with her sweater pulled up around her neck and her pants rolled down to her ankles. Her belly rises, tight as a beach ball.

"Touch it," she says.

What was God thinking about when he made us like this? She's a good person, but all this love, all this touching we seem to need. I've got on my new white suit I bought yesterday, and I feel like a fool. I'm not rational this morning, and it's getting worse by the minute. I don't know how to tell her.

"You don't believe I could do something terrible," Marge says. "But if you don't touch me now, you might find out."

I bought a white-on-white silk tie to go with the suit, because the salesman said it made me look like a famous person.

"You better get sincere," Marge says, "or it's all over between us."

"I should have been at the store an hour ago."

"You don't care about me and the baby," she says.

I do, but I don't know how to explain. She wants Muzak love, with hundreds of violins, and I won't give it to her, and so it goes. I also don't understand myself. I used to be a rational man and now all of a sudden it's white suits and wanting deep down inside to look like a famous person. Any famous person. And also there's Candy. Where will it end? Marge is crying big transparent tears, looking me in the eye without forgiveness. Something is going on here which I don't understand.

"Put your ear down there just once," she says. "Tell me what it sounds like."

What it sounds like is a Dixieland band. Trombones, screechy trumpets, feet stomping. If there is truly a child of mine in there he must be going out of his mind with the noise. I can hear snare drums rolling. I can feel things move.

"Want me to make you breakfast?" Marge says. "There's some fresh fruit in the icebox."

I wonder what the kid will think about this world when he gets out. If he's under the impression it's dark in *there*, wait till he gets a look at the place where I have to live every day. The worst part of living is the uncertainty. It's what makes us all do funny things, like waiting until we're forty-one years old to buy a white suit.

"I'll get a cup of coffee at the store," I tell Marge.

She looks at me like she's been betrayed again.

"I hope it tastes good," she says nastily.

Out there in the sunshiny streets the Cubans are making dope deals and shooting each other. The cops are going berserk in Miami. If you get a traffic ticket it's vital to keep both hands in plain sight, or the officer could get twitchy and blow your head off before you might say hello. I probably *look* like a dope dealer anyway. Did I mention I bought armadillo boots with three-inch heels to go with the suit?

"Listen to it again," Marge says. "Just one more time and then you can go to the damn store."

I put my ear down to her stomach. I still hear music.

This time it sounds like "Won't You Come Home, Bill
Bailey." This child's going to come out crazy for sure.
"Sweetheart," I say, "I can stay home for a while if
you want to talk about this." But her eyes have become
dreamy and distant and I can see she's listening to
something more interesting than her husband.
"Honey," I say. "Marge."
"Go on to the store," she says.
On my way out the front door I get a glimpse of
myself in the big mirror. Besides the suit, etc., my hair
is too long and my face looks desiccated; it's starting to
crack here and there. As if reason, which has been
holding it together for all these years, has decided to
give up and go fishing.
The heat at ten in the morning is already like stepping into a phone booth full of fat people. It takes five
minutes for the air-conditioning to get my Cadillac cool
and by then I'm like the big river from toes to armpits.
The sun is banging on the roof like a bony fist and
shooting flames in my eyes through the tinted windshield. It's partly this awful unrelenting heat that
makes people down here so quick to hate each other.
Move us all to Portland or Des Moines and we'd love
each other like Christians.
The store is full of senior citizens and hippies, as
always at this time of morning; they're eying each
other like dogs in a cage while they look for their little
bargains in the dented canned goods and the day-old
bread rack. Jerry, my vegetable man, is talking to an
old lady in toreador pants and hair-curlers. She's waving a bunch of asparagus in his face as if she's getting
ready to beat him with it. Jerry's worked for me six
years; he came up from stockboy but he'll never rise
higher. He doesn't hate anybody; even the winos, the
shoplifters, the crazies, the women who poke holes in

his melons with greedy thumbs get the same sappy vegetable love from him.

In the back office Candy is waiting for me, sitting behind the big Selectric, reading Wallace Stevens. Her lipstick and sweater are both the same exact shade of lavender. She makes funny mouths over the poetry, runs her tongue over her teeth, narrows her eyes. She reads like some people wrestle; she gets involved.

"So?" I say.

"So nothing," she says. "You look like the Emperor of Ice Cream."

"Don't you have any work to do?"

"Nope."

"Pretend," I tell her. "Or at least read something purely trashy like a normal secretary, so you don't scare the salesmen if they come back here."

I step back into my little private room and stare for a while at the glossy photo on my wall. Me and Bebe Rebozo and you-know-who eating stone crabs together like old friends at the Top of the Hilton. It used to be half the businessmen in this town had a picture like that on their wall; everybody else took them down but I kept mine.

Candy sticks her head in the door.

"What?" I say. "Is somebody here?"

"Nope."

I wait for her to go away so I can go back to trying to figure out how a kid like me ended up in Miami selling groceries for a living. It's a mystery. I went to the High School of Music and Art. I was going to be a violinist, or maybe a painter.

"It's Marge on the phone," Candy says. "Are you here yet?"

"I probably got hung up in traffic," I tell her.

"Oke," she says. "Won't she try to call you on the car phone?"

"I won't be there, will I?"

"Nope."

"Let me know when I do get here."

She stares at me for a second, taking in the suit and the armadillo boots, which I have propped up on my desk. "I thought you and Marge were having a baby," she says.

"She's having the baby. I'm just standing by."

Candy leans forward over my desk and offers one breast through the lavender sweater.

"Touch it," she says.

That's how my life goes any more—in circles. Like somebody is swinging me around his head on a long string. I hear the same things over and over; I see the same things. I get dizzier.

At the Kopper Kettle I order the businessman's special: one tired scoop of tuna served on a lettuce leaf that looks like an old dollar bill, with cottage cheese and half a canned peach. The place is full of old men gobbling this up with unnatural energy. I think I'm the only one under seventy years of age, except for the counterman, a sharply dressed young Cuban who is clearly there for the sake of the electric hate he generates out of these old geezers. It's better for them than an injection of monkey glands. It makes them feel young and tough like they never were when they lived in Boston or Kew Gardens. At least two of them that I can see are wearing shoulder holsters under their polyester jackets.

I study myself in the mirror behind the Cuban and decide that if I look like a famous person it isn't Robert Redford.

The old boy next to me is leaning out of his stool staring at my boots. "What kind of skin is that made out of?" he says.

I can see the butt of a .38 Special sticking out behind the lapel of his coat—not as nasty as the .44 Magnum I keep in the glove box of the Cadillac, but enough to write paid-in-full to anybody's life story.

"Armadillo," I tell him.

"Never did like them beasts," he says. "Remind me of big sow-beetles."

"Too many bugs down here," I tell him. "That's the price we pay for all the good weather."

"Something else I don't like," he whispers loudly. "Cubans."

The counterman is used to this. He catches my eye and winks. "Nice suit, man," he says.

The old boy is still leaning; I'm afraid he's going to fall off the stool; he's galvanized by this hate, he loves it more than life. His plastic teeth are clicking with the happiness of having insulted somebody.

"Who do you think I look like?" I ask the Cuban.

He doesn't know, but I can see he respects the suit. He brings me a refill for my coffee; I don't even have to ask.

The old boy still isn't moving; the armadillo boots have put a hoodoo on him and he's paralyzed, swaying in the breeze from the air-conditioner.

A car backfires, or somebody shoots somebody else out in the street, and breaks the spell. The old boy blinks like he's seeing me for the first time. He holds out his hand, palm up, the way you'd offer it to a dog.

"You think you're so damn smart just because you're not old," he says. "Touch that."

I touch his hand; it's like laying my fingers on the big Selectric in my office when Candy's got it switched on.

It won't stop trembling. If that string they're whirling me around on ever breaks I'll never stop flying until I hit Brazil or somewhere even farther down the line. "Think about it," the old man says.

I think about it while I'm driving the Cadillac back to the store. I'm behind a city bus; the exhaust is coming in through the air-conditioner; it smells vaguely like geraniums. The car phone buzzes. This machine has everything I could get the dealer to put in it. Lord I love my luxuries.

"Hello, sweetheart," I say.

My store is in the bad part of Miami, or what used to be the bad when there was still a good part. About half a mile down the road is a warehouse I've been thinking of buying and making into another store. If I expanded like crazy for about five years and then sold out I could retire down in Brazil or someplace, until the terminal shakes took over.

"Listen to this," Marge says. I know what she's going to do. The bus pulls over and I go around it, phone crammed in my ear.

No more snare drums. Gentle bebop now, a soft tenor sax trying out some phrases. Maybe the kid's asleep. I could have been an artist. God knows what I could have been. Something special.

Marge comes back to the phone. "Do you love me?" she says.

"I've got no time to talk now," I tell her. "I'm back at the store already; I have to take care of business."

Do I love her? I know what she wants—violins and sobbing trombones: Muzak love. She should call Jerry the vegetable man, not me. What I could honestly say she doesn't want to hear.

Last week Candy and I stayed late at the store like we

do sometimes to count the money and make sure nobody's cheating. We spread the cash in piles on the floor in the back room so we could count it better. We made stacks of tens, twenties, fifties, hundreds on my yellow carpet; it looked like a garden in May—Social Security checks and payroll checks and welfare checks to give it a little extra color. She was wearing her pink outfit and had her hair down. We got on our hands and knees and she licked her finger to make the bills behave. After a while we did the necessary thing. You can't fight half a million years of selective breeding even if you think you're a civilized man, and it's better not to try. Candy and I made like beasts in the middle of the currency; when it was over we got up again with tens, twenties, etc. sticking to our sweaty flesh. It felt sincere. You-know-who and his friend Bebe stared down at us from the wall and I was glad I'd never taken them down. A man wants friends who understand him for what he is.

When I first got the store it made me feel like a big man to pull the Cadillac into my own parking stall, with my name spelled out on the curb in yellow paint. Today it makes me feel old and I wish I hadn't spoken to Marge like that on the phone. She can't help wanting what she wants.

I've no sooner sat down at my desk than Candy comes in to say that she is on the phone again. In the corner the Muzak machine is spinning out its tapes and I can hear the sound through the open doors, urging the customers to buy more, putting them in a better mood. Sappy tunes played by a hundred violins, music reduced to rubble and mud.

"I'm leaving you," Marge says before I can get out a hello. "There's no sincerity in you any more and I don't want to live with you."

The doors are open wide enough to let me see a slice

of the store while I listen to Marge telling me what a no-good I am. Jerry is setting out watermelons. I like him like a son, but he'll never amount to anything until he learns to hate a little, like everybody else down here in this crazy town.

"You're nothing," Marge says. I want to agree with her, or at least explore the possibility, but she doesn't give me the chance. "Why should I spend any more time on you? A nothing person."

Jerry is sprinkling the lettuce with a hose to make it look fresher than it is. He knows lettuce, he knows spinach, rutabagas, turnips, carrots, zucchini, six kinds of melons, even the exotics, but about life he knows next to nothing at all.

"I've already packed my suitcase," Marge says.

The violins are humming like bees; if I leaned a little farther I'm sure I could see customers waltzing from the canned olives to the mushrooms, soft-shoeing between the freezer cases, buying, buying. Five years ago it was fun to watch this; now I'd like to throw them all out of the store, tell them to go home and learn to behave like people.

"Sweetheart," I say to Marge, "it's your life and I'd be the last to want to interfere, but I'd say you ought to think it over."

"Forget it," she says.

"All right. Have a good trip. Send me a postcard and a picture of the kid after he's born and I'll send you a little check from time to time to help out."

She hangs up with a bang that leaves my ear ringing. I suppose I deserve it.

"How can you be such a son of a bitch?" Candy wants to know.

"How many times did I tell you not to listen in on my private phone calls?"

"You're no better than him," she says, pointing to the

jowly man sitting between me and Bebe Rebozo in the photograph. "Anyway, I'm your secretary; I'm supposed to know everything that goes on in your life."
"You don't suspect even a tenth of it," I tell her. "Are you still seeing your crazy boyfriend?"
"Which one?"
"The poet. The one that beats you."
"He's really a very sweet guy," she says. "The only time he hits me is when he's feeling terrible about the world."
"And you put up with that? You like it?"
She shrugs, causing delicious movements under the lavender sweater. "It's interesting."
I can understand. Hate is invigorating. Necessary, even. But every time I try to explain this to Marge she shakes her head. If I insist she puts her fingers in her ears and starts humming a Muzak tune to drown me out.
"Why don't you leave him?" I tell Candy. "Let's run off together. We could go to Brazil."
"You're always saying that, but you don't mean it."
"How do you know?"
She shrugs again. "You'd hate Brazil," she says.
There's a growing noise out in the store. People yelling. She sticks her head out to see what's going on. "I think Jerry needs you," she says.
My vegetable man is having a tug-of-war with a hippie. Each of them has hold of one end of a watermelon and they're dancing in the aisle between the cucumbers and the pyramids of oranges, yanking on that enormous fruit like the two women in front of King Solomon. The long-haired boy is breathing hard through his mouth. Jerry's face is red and furious: the first time in six years I've seen him angry. Maybe there's some hope for him after all.

"I want to buy it," the long-hair says. "Are you the manager? He won't let me buy it." He'd be a pleasant-looking kid if it wasn't for the wispy beard and the pushed-out lower lip like a two-year-old when somebody's taken away his candy.

"It's too beautiful," Jerry says to me. "It's not for him."

He's shouting and people are beginning to gather round, looking pleased and interested. It's a different crowd than the morning people; these folks are more respectable, better-dressed, more in tune with the world. It doesn't prevent them from gathering to see the fight.

The kid looks me up and down without letting go of the melon. "Are you really the manager?" he says. "You look more like you're in the Mafia or something, with that suit. What kind of boots are those?"

I can outstare a kid like that any day of the week. "If you don't let go of that melon I'm going to call a friend of mine and arrange to have your legs broken," I tell him. "Give it to me."

He does. It really is the most beautiful watermelon in the world, tender deep-green, with lighter-colored stripes. It weighs at least forty pounds. A giant. Unique.

"Don't let him buy it," Jerry says. "Don't give it to him."

The Muzak is playing a maple-syrup version of "Canadian Sunset." It gives me strength to do what I have to do. I heave the melon up above my head and hold it there, looking at Jerry and the kid. I know how Solomon felt at this moment.

"No," Jerry says.

My arms are quivering but I could hold it up there forever. I look at the kid to see what he thinks. He shakes his head. "Man . . ." he says.

I'm thinking of Candy on her hands and knees among the fifty-dollar bills; I'm thinking of Marge at home packing her suitcases and getting ready to take my kid away. Somebody in the crowd behind me says, "Crazy," softly.

"You can't," Jerry says. But he has to learn about life; I'm going to help him.

I throw the melon down. It goes off at my feet like a vegetable blockbuster. My armadillo boots are ruined; my white pants are red juice, black seeds, and bits of broken pink meat all the way to the crotch; my white jacket is crying pink tears. If I look like a famous person now, it's Soupy Sales.

"You count the money tonight," I tell Candy. "I'm going home."

In the awful heat inside the Cadillac I smell myself; it's like a tropical paradise gone sour, but I don't care. I'm feeling happy. I cut off a city bus at the traffic light and the sound of his horn is like music. I'm thinking about Candy, I'm thinking about Brazil.

I'm thinking about Marge while I'm stopped at the next light, when something fetches my rear bumper a hard whack. I look in the mirror and it's the bus I cut off; the son of a bitch got insulted. I turn off down a side street but he's still coming, bent on vengeance. Me, I love this hate because it's relentless and pure. But it's time to flee.

There's a Yellow Cab waiting outside my front door, but no sign of Marge. I tap on the window and slip the driver a ten-dollar bill. "No need to wait," I tell him. "The lady changed her mind."

My wife is in our bedroom, throwing last-minute things into a suitcase; two more are stacked by the door, ready to go.

"What happened to you?" she says, eying the suit.

"Never mind that," I tell her. "Come and sit in the living room with me; I want to explain some things." She's beside me on the couch; her belly is bigger than ever; if I look close I can see it give little jumps under her dress.

"Love is an easy thing," I tell her. "Being a son of a bitch is harder but it's the best thing we've got."

"No, no, no," she says.

"I don't mean you can't love also, but that comes after."

She sticks her fingers in her ears and stands up; I try to come after her but she's dancing around the room, humming "Hello, Young Lovers" as loud as she can, trying to drown out what I think is wisdom.

"Touch me," I say.

I come up beside her and take her around the waist; we're dancing together, working up a sweat; the kid is probably thinking it's an earthquake, the end of the world. She's stopped humming but we dance and dance, to no music except the soft shuffle of our feet over the blue carpet. We weave in and out of the lemon-colored slices of Florida sunlight coming through the cracks in the curtains. She puts her arms around my neck; I lean forward over the curve of her belly and kiss her on the cheek.

"If you won't hate, how can you love?" I whisper.

She dances away from me, whirling and swooping around the furniture. But sooner or later she'll have to stop and listen. I'm going to save everybody from this Muzak love if they'd only give me a chance.

It Could Happen

Segal slumps at the table, eyes more than half closed, thinking he'd rather be home. His head feels like the inside of a soggy sandwich. Across from him Korda holds the deck almost hidden in one big hand, knuckles folded over the cards. Next to him Katzman waits for the deal. Katzman's eyes are a little crazy; he loves poker, loves to win big. The new player looks at the deuce of clubs lying on the table in front of him and frowns. Segal can't quite remember his name—it's a color, he thinks. White? Green? Whatever his name is, he's the heavy loser; two, maybe three hundred dollars, Segal figures. Four of the man's checks are in front of Korda, held down by heavy piles of red chips. Segal feels sorry for him, but it's three in the morning and he's too tired to worry about winners and losers.

He sneaks another look at Katzman and decides he doesn't know yet. He's hostile, but he's always hostile on Tuesday nights with money on the table. Katzman is the kind of player who slams down a winning hand and laughs at the losers. Segal is certain that Shannon hasn't told him yet.

"You going to bet, Jack?" Korda says to him.

"No," he says. "I can't even see the cards any more; I think I'll go home."

"You can't break up the game now," the new man says. He looks puzzled and grieved, as if he can't believe his bad luck.

"The rest of you can keep playing," Segal says. He feels sorry for Green or White or whatever his name is, but he has other things to think about. Ever since Shannon happened to him he's felt his life revolving slowly around him, demanding patience, full of sudden sounds and flashes of strong color like a Kabuki drama. He wants to get in his car and think slowly and carefully about his situation while he makes the long drive home along the San Diego Freeway.

"We can't quit now," the new man says.

From the other side of the table Flowers blinks at him through gold-rimmed glasses. "Maybe you ought to," he says. "You're not doing so well."

"Second-best hands," Green or White says. "It can't go on like that all night."

"Just bad luck," Korda says. "Happens to everybody."

Katzman laughs. He laughs like a Cossack, Segal thinks. When he finds out, God knows what he'll do. It can't help but be ugly. Maybe he'll beat her. With a man like that, who can tell.

In the chair next to Flowers, Roth is nodding, half asleep himself. He's the night's other serious loser, a terrible poker player, but he loves the game and he can afford to lose; he's a stockbroker and this year people are buying. The Dow-Jones is floating up like a hot-air balloon and Roth is sitting in the basket, making money faster than he can spend it. There's no need to feel sorry for Roth.

Korda walks him out to the car. "What do you know about this guy Green?" he says.

"What's to know?" Segal says. "If you're worried about the checks, ask Katzman. He brought him."

"He doesn't look right," Korda says.

"Maybe he can't afford to lose so much. Maybe you ought to make him quit."

"He's a grown man," Korda says. "I'm not his keeper."

He leans into the Buick through the open driver's window; his breath smells like beer and cigarettes and Segal is tempted to shut off the car and walk back in to play some more, but it's too late, he's too tired to care how the cards come out, he wants to drive, listen to the radio, watch his life revolve. "Next Tuesday," he says. Driving the freeways is a spiritual experience. Segal floats above the city lights like a dream of himself, leaning back against the velour seat, touching the wheel with his fingertips, feeling the endless curve and recurve of this concrete track that carves through the Valley like a dead river. To get himself in the proper stance he says his name over and over—Jack Segal, Jack Segal, Jack Segal—until signified falls into signifier like a planet diving into a black hole and only the sign is left to be him. He sails along the white concrete like a blank page with his name at the top, waiting to be written. Jack Segal.

He catches himself thinking about the store. Surely Minnie is stealing from the cash register. He hasn't actually seen her, but the receipts are short at the end of the day—sometimes five dollars and fifty cents, sometimes ten and change, never an even figure. If he asks her she rolls her fat shoulders and says, "Hell, Mr. Jack, you know I wouldn't do something like that. What you picking on me for? Maybe you don't like black people? Is that it?" And now she's seen him with Shannon and he can't even ask about the money any more, because she smiles her little *I know you now Mr. Bad Man* smile. What's ten bucks compared to being in love with a fourteen-year-old girl, in God's scale of sinful behavior? So as he shoots down this dead river saying Jack Segal, Jack Segal to himself, what he sees is Minnie's teeth, her little mean smile, her knowledge that Segal is a bad man.

2

After Shannon the store is what Jack Segal loves best. He loves the shelves, the bins, the racks, the records in their candy-colored jackets, the two wide windows that look out on Ocean Boulevard where the tourists and the surfers and the street people pass. He knows that one of these days the Great Quake will come and the whole street will tumble down the Palisades into the wide Pacific, and that makes his love stronger. He's conscious that he's looking into Eternity out those windows, but inside his store he's King Jack. Or he was until Minnie caught him in the storeroom with Shannon. All he was doing was holding the girl's hand and looking into her violet eyes, but that was enough.

This morning Minnie's smile is more knowing than ever. "You got to get more New Wave, Mr. Jack," she says. "This red-neck stuff ain't going to sell." She's waving a Doc Watson album in Jack's face. Doc's funny hat and string tie make Jack want to cry, that and the way he's holding his fiddle cramped under his chin as if it was the only thing in the world worth doing.

"How long we had this one?" Minnie says. "Two years now? How you going to make any money like that, Mr. Jack? You better to get with it or you going to lose this place and then what you going to do?"

Segal turns his back to her and shuffles through the records in the bargain bin. Bob Brookmeyer. Pete Fountain. Toshiko Akyoshi. Nothing anybody would buy in a thousand years. The jackets are coming loose at the corners; he knows he might as well throw them all in the trash and take a tax loss but he hasn't the heart. Where he wants to be is on the beach with Shannon but she's in school and won't be around until three o'clock.

Customers come and customers go. He sells Air Supply, the B-52's, Police, Fleetwood Mac. A black kid, thinner than thin, comes wheeling through the door with a Walkman pinned to his head. "No roller skates in the store," Segal says. The kid's eyes stay unfocused. "No roller skates," Segal shouts. The kid throws him a single glance of pure hate and spins out the door again into the street where morning sunlight is beating down the sidewalks like hail.

"What you got against black people, Mr. Jack?"

"Why don't you go clean the back room?" he says. "It looks like there's been an earthquake. Nobody can find anything back there. And sweep out while you're at it."

At eleven Korda calls and wants to have lunch. "The Fish Grotto," he says.

"Why?" Segal says.

"What, *why?* Because I want to talk to you, that's why."

Behind the Fish Grotto's aquarium walls grotesque sea-creatures float with open mouths, watching the eaters eat.

"Look at that thing," Korda says. "Can a thing like that exist?"

It has a head like a gargoyle, stubby spikes for fins, a tail like a bad illustration of Moby Dick. Two bulbous intelligent eyes stare at Segal through the glass, seeing a bad man.

"So this girl you're going out with," Korda says. He breaks a roll, butters it, sticks it in his mouth. Korda owns a construction company, combs his hair like Johnny Cash, has knuckles the size of walnuts. He's the best poker player in the group, without Katzman's weakness for pushing a good hand when it's obvious somebody has a better one.

"What girl?" Segal says. "Who told you?"

"Minnie. I was at the store looking for you last week and she told me. She's worried about you, Jack."

"She should worry about herself."

"What are you doing with this girl? Is it love or what?"

"This is what you wanted to talk about?"

"I'm just thinking what sense does it make, a man your age and a thirteen-year-old girl."

"Fourteen," Segal says.

"So fourteen. Jack, it ain't healthy. Not civilized, you know what I mean."

"Who made you my father?"

Korda draws back and looks at the half-eaten roll in his hand as if he's never seen it before. Behind him the impossible fish hangs in the water, watching Jack with blue-gray eyes big as ping-pong balls. Korda sighs. "All right, all right, none of my business. But we've been friends for a long time. Every Tuesday night you come, I watch you lose your money, I don't say anything. You don't play well, but you like the game, all right. It's your money. How much fun do we get out of life? But this is different."

"Leave it alone," Segal says.

"What do you do, you and this Shannon? Are you making it with her? Who is she?"

Segal feels like he has to tell somebody. It can't be Minnie, it might as well be Korda. "Katzman's daughter," he says.

"Don't make jokes," Korda says.

Segal shakes his head. "No joke."

Korda whistles. "Does he know?"

"Not yet."

"So what do you do with her?"

"We talk."

"What do you mean, talk?"

"You don't know what talk is? You move the mouth, words come out. We talk."

Korda thinks about it while he finishes his roll. "Fourteen-year-old girls don't know *how* to talk," he says.

"Sometimes I think she's a hundred years old," Segal says. "She's smart. She knows things. She's not like the others."

"All right," Korda says. "So you talk. You don't touch her. Maybe it's love. But how old are you, thirty-three?"

"Thirty-six."

"Thirty-six and fourteen," Korda says. "So how long could it last? Don't tell me about the Supreme Court judge and that senator from South Carolina, or those movie actors that marry little girls. You own a record store—it's not the same thing, right? Businessmen is what we are, Jack. Not senators, not movie actors. For us life is the real thing. No fantasies. How long before she finds herself some good-looking kid from Muscle Beach with a body like you and I never had, and he starts to do more than talk?"

"It's not going to happen," Segal says. "This is different."

3

Segal watches the clock, eager for the afternoon to run by and for Shannon to come. He watches Minnie watching him. So if I was in the movies it wouldn't be wrong, he thinks. If I was a judge on the Supreme Court everybody would say *Isn't it wonderful—a man like that with all his dignity and he can still love like a regular human being.* Because I run a record store it isn't allowed.

"How was lunch, Mr. Jack?" Minnie's standing in the door to the back room, holding her broom like a spear at rest. A tough lady. Maybe she steals because she has to, Segal thinks. How much do I pay her? What do I know about her family? Maybe she has six or eight kids at home and needs the money to buy milk, bread, meat. Maybe my sin is bigger than hers.

"Lunch was lunch," he says. "How about the back room?"

"Want to look, Mr. Jack?"

He shakes his head no. Maybe her man cheats on her with some little girl who laughs like a bird and has breasts like hard apples. Maybe he takes her paycheck to buy dope.

"How much do I pay you?" he says.

"Now, Mr. Jack, you ain't going to start that business about the cash register again, are you?"

"No," he says. "How much?"

"Ain't you the one who signs my check? Four dollars and fifty cents an hour."

"It's not enough," Segal says. "From today I'm giving you a raise. Five-fifty an hour."

She shakes her head at him sadly. "You think that's going to make it all right, Mr. Jack?"

"I'm not a bad man," he says. "I'm just trying to get along. To live, you understand that?"

"You don't like black folks, Mr. Jack. You think if you give me another dollar here and there, that's going to make everything just fine?"

"You want the raise?" Segal says. "Yes or no?"
"Just so long as you know it won't make no difference," she tells him.
"Who'd know better than me?" Segal says.
"What's right is right, Mr. Jack. Ain't that what life is?"
What life is I don't know, Segal thinks. He watches Minnie push her broom down the aisle between Classical and Blues; her straight-held back is like a reproach, worse than her smile. The dust she kicks up into the sunbeams is like ashes.

4

When Shannon comes in, Minnie is behind the register taking money from an old man who's clutching three records from the bargain bin. He's holding the torn covers under his arm as if they were infinitely precious while he fumbles in a little change purse for the quarters and half-dollars to give to Minnie.
"I'll be back in an hour," Segal says.
He walks hand in hand with Shannon down the Santa Monica Pier, not saying anything, feeling only the great pleasure of her fingers curled into his palm. Illicit, he thinks, illegal even, but oh God it feels so fine. His heart is leaping like a live bird knocking behind his ribs, pumping joy down to his toes. What's wisdom compared to this, he thinks. Here's life—I'm drowning in it.
They sit on the bench at the sea end of the pier, facing out on the Pacific. Mouth like a little rose, Segal thinks. He hears Korda speaking sternly at lunch while the sea-monsters watched from behind the glass. *You're*

making a fool of yourself with this girl. He doesn't want to know. His lips are trembling. More than anything he's ever wanted in this life Segal wants to lean over and kiss her, but he's no movie actor, no Supreme Court judge—he can't be kissing a girl less than half his age in public. No fantasies, he tells himself sternly.

"What's the matter with you, Jack?" Shannon says. "You look like you want to do something."

"I want to kiss you," Segal says.

"So go ahead."

"Not here."

"Sometimes you act like an old man," she says. She pinches his leg hard enough to make him jump. "I don't like it when you act old," she says.

"No fantasies," he says.

"Who's a fantasy? Me? Touch me. What are you afraid of?"

"Life," Segal tells her.

She looks at him seriously. "Yeah," she says. "Well anyway I told him."

Segal looks at her without understanding. "Told who?"

"My father."

"About us?"

"About life," Shannon says. "Don't be dull, Jack. I don't like dull. Wake up."

I guess he had to know sooner or later, Segal thinks.

"You're coming to dinner Saturday," she says. "He wants to talk to you."

"What did he say when you told him?"

He wants to put his arms around her; instead he folds his hands in his lap, thinking about Katzman. He's a lout, Segal thinks, a gross man, a *macher*, a Cossack. But he never did me any wrong, so what am I doing to him?

"He shouted and he slammed the doors like he always does when I do something he doesn't like, and then he called up the rabbi. But I don't think the rabbi said anything to make him feel better."

"I understand how he feels," Segal says. "If I had a daughter . . ."

"You're talking like an old man again," Shannon says.

All around them old men and children are dangling long lines off the pier, hoping to hook fish as exotic and beautiful as those at the Fish Grotto, but Segal doesn't see them. Sunlight beats the water like a flail, making little fires burn and die on the waves, but Segal doesn't see the sun either.

"What are we going to do?" he says.

"Let's walk on the beach. I get tired of sitting here all the time."

He takes off his shoes and rolls up his pants and they walk the edge of the water among the near-nakeds and the crazies and the simply hopeful. A man in a red bikini bottom and a Superman cape runs by them, flapping his arms; two women playing backgammon in the shade of a striped umbrella look up at Jack with suspicion; farther down the beach four men are flying fighting kites, big gaudy paper birds that swoop and slash at each other.

"See?" Shannon says. "Everybody else is crazy too, so why not us?"

She runs ahead of Segal and does graceful cartwheels in the wet sand. When she comes back to him she holds up her mouth; her eyes are half-closed. He bends down and kisses her; the crazies and hopefuls look on.

"What's the matter with you, Jack?" she says.

5

The next day Segal doesn't feel like there's anything the matter with him, except that his head is filled with lumpy cottonwool, like an old mattress. He can't think. He eats, but it doesn't taste like anything. He drinks but he's still thirsty. He's not sick, he's just in love, he tells himself, humming the tune through a dry throat. Flowers calls and asks him to lunch, but Segal knows Korda put him up to it and says no; the next day Roth calls and gets the same answer.

"I know what I'm doing is dumb," Segal tells him, clutching the phone with a damp hot hand, "but it's what I'm doing. No lectures. No sermons. I don't want advice. Whose life is it? Mine. So I'm living it."

Behind him Minnie is waving the feather duster over the shelves of records, raising clouds of the fine beach dust that comes in under the door, around the sealed windows, floats in ´ with the customers. Segal knows she's listening.

"Do I take you to dinner and tell you it's crazy to get rich with the stock market?" he says to Roth. "That's different? Why is it different? Because it's respectable? All right, then, I'm not respectable. But you haven't seen her eyes, her mouth, her hair. Maybe you wouldn't think respectable is so important."

Clouds of beach dust, fine as fine flour, shot with sunlight, settle around his head. Yesterday Shannon told him that at the very instant the sun goes below the ocean a ray of clear green light streaks under the water for a fraction of a fraction of a second. Thirty-six years of living on the edge of Pacific and Segal's never seen it.

"Have you ever seen the green ray?" he asks Minnie.

She pauses with the duster above her head. "The what, Mr. Jack?"

"The green ray."

She shakes her head. "It ain't none of my business, Mr. Jack, but I think you're getting crazy. You ought to be listening to your friends and doing like they say."

"None of you know a goddamn thing," Segal says.

"Let them introduce you to some nice woman your age," Minnie says. "Somebody that could make you happy."

On Friday morning it's Korda again. Segal starts to hang up. "Wait," Korda says. "This is business."

"What business? I don't know anything about construction."

"Not construction. The game. There's something we have to do. I want you to come along—it'll take you out of yourself. I'll pick you up at the store in half an hour."

While he waits Segal sits down with the accounts. It isn't as bad as Minnie makes out. People come, people buy. With the prime rate coming down he can afford to get a little deeper into the bank, buy more stock. Classical always sells. For the new stuff he'll take Minnie's advice. The books say he'll clear thirty, thirty-five thousand this year. Not enough to live like a movie actor, but enough to get by.

When Korda's white four-door Lincoln pulls up, Segal peers in and sees Katzman in the passenger seat; in the back seat is Green, looking unhappy. His face is pinched and pale.

"Get in," Korda says.

The Lincoln moves in the traffic as easily as a dead leaf floating downstream; Korda drives with his fingertips, as graceful as when he deals the cards.

"Our man Green here gave us some rubber checks," Korda says. "Four hundred and eighty-five dollars worth. Some bad streak he was on. Also he can't play poker too well. Now it turns out he doesn't even have twenty bucks in his account at the bank."

The Lincoln is floating down Venice Boulevard, weaving in and out between vans full of hippies and surfers, past cop cars and buses, catching the lights on orange, slipping through gaps in the traffic that aren't there.

"I thought I was going to have it for you," Green says.

"You will," Korda says. "Don't worry yourself, my friend."

"What's this all about?" Segal says. "What are we doing?" When he shifts his eyes to look at Korda the sockets feel full of sand. His head feels like it's floating six inches above his shoulders, with no neck intervening.

Korda swings the Lincoln into a parking lot full of fat cars and gaudy pickups. "Here's the first one," he says. "Get in there and do your stuff."

"What is this?" Segal says.

"Mr. Green is going to go into this supermarket and cash a check for me," Korda says. "And then we'll take him to another one, until I've got my four hundred and eighty-five bucks. Then we'll take him home."

"Cashing bad checks is a felony in California," Segal says.

Korda smiles his Johnny Cash smile. "That's his problem."

"I'm not going to do it," Green says. "You can't make me do something illegal."

Korda's smile is gentle but the menace hangs in the car like thick smoke. "You want to bet?" He leans over the seat and reaches out with one heavy finger. "Go on," he says.

"What would you do if he didn't go?" Segal says. Green is already disappearing through the automatic doors of the market.

"That's why you're not a poker player," Korda says. "You don't *think* right."

Katzman laughs his Cossack laugh. His eyes are a little crazy; it's his Tuesday-night face. "Lucky at love, unlucky at cards," he says. He turns to Korda. "My daughter," he says. "Jack here is coming to dinner at my house tomorrow night to tell me how come he's going out with my fourteen-year-old girl. What do you think of that?"

"I already told him what I think," Korda says. "But this is business."

"That's business too," Katzman says. "Monkey business. Movie-actor business. A little girl."

"I don't want to talk about it now," Segal says.

Katzman closes his eyes. "So tomorrow night," he says. "I'll ask the questions and you better have some answers, Mr. Segal."

6

Anybody could live my life better than I could, Segal thinks, staring across the table at Louis and Dolores Katzman. On the plate in front of him is a grapefruit with a cherry in the middle.

"Eat," Dolores says. "Don't be shy, Jack. What happened to you could happen to anybody."

"To a sensible man it couldn't happen," her husband says. The Cossack's mustache is broad and heavy and turned down at the corners. He's in real estate and the Katzman house is a fantasy of turrets and towers and spiral stairs that lead to unknown places, perched on a hill in Sherman Oaks.

"How long has it been going on?" Katzman says. The mustache moves up and down when he talks.

"Three months," Segal says. "Where's Shannon? I thought she was going to be here tonight."

"I told her to go to the movies," Katzman says. "So three months. The question I ask is what have you been doing."

"Nothing. We talk. We hold hands."

"Love could happen to anybody," Dolores Katzman says. She is smaller than her daughter. Her face is set in sad lines.

Katzman spoons up a bite of grapefruit and chews it slowly. "When her mother heard, she locked herself in her room for three days," he tells Segal. "I had to bring her meals on a tray."

"I'm sorry," Segal says.

"It was just the shock," Dolores says. "A surprise, you know what I mean."

"Don't apologize to him," Katzman says.

"He's nice," Dolores says. "You can see he didn't take advantage."

"At his age falling in love with a little girl I call taking advantage already."

"Happens what happens," Dolores says. "Eat, Jack. This is not the inquisition. A friendly dinner, talking things over like adult people. At least he's not a crazy person," she tells Katzman.

"Because he wears a tie?"

"He owns a store, it's not like he was a movie actor."

"True," Katzman says. "I want to be fair. He owns a

store, he owns a house, he's not a lowlife like the people you read about in the newspapers who get little girls to come into their cars so they can touch them."

"Calm down," Dolores says. "Your voice always gets too loud when you're excited."

"I'm not excited," Katzman says. "A man comes to my house and tells me he's going out with my little girl that's just a freshman in high school, but I'm not excited."

"Let him eat," Dolores says. "You can see he means well."

Embarrassed, Segal fumbles with his grapefruit. He imagines the sorrow of being married to Katzman for a lifetime; he'd like to comfort Dolores but this doesn't seem like the right moment.

"So," Katzman says. "You're going to tell me what? You love my daughter and it's all pure and holy and I don't have any right to talk?"

"You have a right," Dolores says.

"Let him speak for himself. Do I have a right or don't I?"

"You have a right," Segal admits. He pushes away the grapefruit, defeated. Under his feet the carpet feels like quicksand; off to his right the Alice-in-Wonderland stairs lead off to unexplored regions. "But it's true Shannon and I love each other." Saying it, he feels a sly triumph; what's Louis the real-estate Cossack going to do about love? Still the girl is fourteen years old, Segal thirty-six—he's doing an enormous thing here. Some people could call it crazy. He wants to explain himself to Katzman but what can he say? Can he tell Katzman about her mouth, her hair, her eyes—deep violet, a color that opens his heart like a knife? He feels that to Katzman this will be no excuse. About himself, then. The businessman. Music-lover. Never married. What a mess I'm making of my life, he thinks, looking at Katzman's angry face. Anybody could live it better.

When Shannon comes in the door he jumps out of his chair, takes her hand, leads her to sit beside him at the table. Katzman glares but the mustache doesn't move; he says nothing. Shannon's hand is hot, dry, alive. Segal looks into her eyes, feels his heart open like a ripe fruit.

"How was the movie?" Dolores says.

"Never mind the damn movie," Katzman says. He shakes a finger at his daughter and at Segal. "Is everybody crazy here but me? It has to stop. No more." He's out of his chair, shouting, making a fist. His eyes are crazy. The mustache is flapping up and down. Segal sees that Shannon is crying, tears rolling down her face like little transparent fish, dying on her blouse. He stands up and opens his mouth. But what's he going to do? Hit Louis Katzman? It's his house, he's her father, he has the right.

"Calm down," Dolores says. "Everybody sit. We're talking like human beings here, not savages."

"No more," Katzman says.

"Sit," Dolores says. "Love is love. It can't be helped."

"Daddy," Shannon says.

"No more," Katzman says.

"Hush," Dolores says.

7

Tuesday night. Segal looks at his cards with despair. Two hearts in the hole, two more face up. Three cards to get the one he needs, but what if it comes? He wins maybe twenty dollars and then what? Will his life be better?

"Raise a dollar," Roth says. Two pairs, Segal thinks sadly, but he'll never fill it. He pushes his money in, waits for the cards to fall.

"So you went with her father to see the rabbi," Korda says. "Then what?"

"Then nothing," Segal says. "We decided we wait two years until she's sixteen, then if we still feel the same way we get married."

"We playing or talking here?" Green says. He's back in the game with fresh cash, bundles of twenty-dollar bills. Nobody asks where they came from.

"Two years is a long time," Korda says. He peels cards off the deck, flips them neatly across the table. The ten of hearts lands in front of Segal. "My advice is don't take it too seriously."

"Pair of kings bets five dollars," Roth says. "How can he not take it seriously? I remember when I was in love."

"When was that?" Flowers says.

"College," Roth says. "I was crazy for this little girl in my political science class. I wrote poems, sent flowers, everything."

"She was beautiful?" Korda says.

"I don't say beautiful. But she had something I had to have. I don't know . . . vitality, spirit, something. When she stood up and answered a question from the professor I thought I was going to die if she didn't love me. I went crazy in my room every night, thinking what she might be doing right then with some other guy. It wasn't good, you know? I was failing my courses—who could read books?"

"Love is a foolishness," Flowers says. "What's the best

that can happen?" The girl says yes, you marry her, after six months you get bored with each other."

"I don't agree," Roth says. "So I failed a couple of classes, but it was worth it. It was beautiful."

"Going crazy is beautiful?" Flowers says.

"Last card," Korda says. He deals them carefully, one by one, face down. Segal lifts up a corner—jack of hearts. In ten years of playing the game he's never had a royal flush before.

"Sure it's beautiful," Roth says. "Is it my bet? How much is in the pot—that's what I'm betting."

8

Segal is suffering. The dry throat, the head full of cottonwool, the feeling of not knowing exactly where he is, have all come back. In bed at three in the morning he thinks *cancer;* after breakfast he thinks *flu;* in the afternoon he thinks *love.* He thinks *two years before I can marry her.* He looks out the two big windows of his store and thinks about the Great Earthquake. He's not sure he doesn't want it to come tomorrow and tumble him, Minnie, the surfers, the tourists, everything in a big struggling heap into the loving foamy waters. It would solve everything.

Every Saturday night he picks up Shannon and takes her out—dinner, dancing, movies, a concert. Always it's Katzman who greets him with nasty eyes, opens the door an inch at a time, makes Segal squeeze past him into the living room where Dolores sits him on the couch, offers candy from a bowl, a cigarette from a pewter box, talks about love as if it was a misfortune which could happen to anybody. She wants better for her daughter than what she got in life, but with Katzman standing there they can't talk about that. Segal eats chocolates and indulges himself imagining the aftermath of the Great Quake, Katzman the survivor ruling Sherman Oaks from his castle on the hill, supplicants making their pleas for mercy to Queen Dolores. "Happens what happens," she says with sad eyes, and Katzman strings up the bad men from the branches of his evergreen trees in the back yard. So why am I thinking apocalypse? Segal asks himself. Because I don't like this world?

"Have a chocolate," Dolores tells him. "Shannon'll be down in a minute; she's making herself pretty for you."

This Saturday night is different from the other Saturday nights. Katzman is waiting for him alone. He opens the door wide for Segal, motions him to the couch. Segal looks around for Dolores but the room is empty.

"I sent them out," Katzman says. "I wanted to talk to you alone; maybe we could understand each other."

"Katzman . . ."

"Call me Louis. It's a beginning." He pulls up a chair, turns it around and straddles it, facing Segal. Dark wiry hairs curl up from under his shirtsleeves and cover the backs of his hands. Too much is too much, Segal thinks. Too much hair, too much flesh: what kind of a man is this?

"What kind of person are you, that's what I asked myself," Katzman says.

"Not good, not bad," Segal says.

"I made inquiries. A detective. He followed you around for two weeks, cost me eighteen hundred dollars which I didn't have. You don't do anything terrible. You run your store, you play a little poker which I knew already, you go home at night and watch television. Your store is doing pretty good—not wonderful but pretty good. Your neighbors don't have anything bad to say. Your friends I didn't bother the detective with—they're my friends too: I know what they think." Segal tries to be angry but he can't do it. Katzman's opened his life like a telegram and all he can feel is that despite the Cossack's mustache, despite the unnatural vigor, he likes the man.

"So I want you to explain to me why this craziness," Katzman says. "Going out with younger women at our age, I can understand. But a girl of fourteen? Does this make sense to you?"

"Not exactly," Segal says.

"I beg you," Katzman says. "I beg you to explain to me so I can understand."

"Love," Segal says. He reaches for the pewter box and takes out a cigarette. Katzman's house is the only place where he smokes.

"Love?" Katzman says.

"Love."

"Segal, that's a word, *love,* not an explanation. The rabbi, he doesn't understand. The social worker I went to and asked if I had to let you see my daughter, she doesn't understand. Nobody understands except maybe you, and if you don't explain it to me, who will? My wife Dolores says *love,* my daughter says *love.* And now you. One word is supposed to explain everything?"

Segal coughs. What with his woolly head, his dry throat, the cigarette is strangling him but he doesn't want to give it up. He takes a deep drag and coughs so hard he has to bend over and put his head between his knees before he can start breathing again. "Listen, Katzman," he says to the carpet. "Why not let us be? It's two years before we can get married. Two years is a long time. Anything could happen. I can't do anything about it; you can't do anything about it. So why not wait and see like civilized people?"

"I don't have to let her see you," Katzman says. "The social worker said I could forbid it."

"So would it be better if Shannon was riding around with some kid on a motorcycle? If she was going to parties with hot tubs and drugs? Is this what you'd want?"

"Oh God," Katzman says. "What am I supposed to do?"

"Do you have anything to drink?" Segal says. "A little bourbon, maybe? Some wine?"

In the kitchen they sit across the table from each other. The whiskey makes Jack's throat feel better but it makes his head swell up. He falls apart from himself and sees the scene from the kitchen ceiling: two men sitting down there, far away from him, talking nonsense.

"Love," Katzman says. The word floats up and bumps against the ceiling like a party balloon. "You don't know what you're getting into, Jack. When I was twenty I was in love with Dolores."

"It's not the same thing," Segal tells him. "You were in love twenty years ago; I'm in love now. That's all the difference in the world."

"I'm trying to keep you from making a mistake like I made when I was young."

"I don't want to know about you and Dolores," Segal says. "Tell me tonight and in the morning you'll hate me because I know."

The ceiling where half of Segal is hanging is full of little sparkles embedded in the dim plaster. Down there two heads bob and weave in conversation, exchanging ideas about life. From up here it looks stupid, but Segal knows if he makes a little effort he'll pop back into the middle of things and it'll be vital, a serious discussion. He's not sure he wants to make the little effort.

"Shannon's a wonderful girl," he says. "I'll be good to her." The part of him that sits across the table from Katzman feels full of righteousness and power. The other half is thinking *jackass, idiot.*

"She's not even old enough to be dating," Katzman says. "What does she know about life?"

"In some countries girls get married when they're twelve," Segal says.

"Do me a favor," Katzman says. "Don't tell me about India."

"Other places too," Segal says.

"Savages. My daughter is not a savage."

But Segal can hear a note of hope in the other man's voice, like a single fiddle string faintly plucked.

"If you were a professor, something like that," Katzman says, "I could understand this craziness. If you were in the movies. But you're a businessman like me."

How warm it is in Katzman's kitchen, Segal thinks. How comfortable! Behind him a refrigerator as big as a garden shed purrs sweetly. Microwave ovens, six-slice toasters, mixers and blenders wait to make whatever Katzman might want. The real-estate Cossack lives like a king already, even before the Great Quake.

"We could understand each other, Jack," Katzman says. He sips his whiskey, wipes the mustache with the back of one hand. "I know what it is to sell things to people who don't want to buy. It's complicated, Jack. People think it's simple but it isn't. We struggle. Every day like a war, am I right?"

"I sell records," Segal says.

Even the chairs in Katzman's kitchen are wonderful;

the bottoms are soft leather that molds itself to Segal as if he was born there, grew up in that seat. The backs curve precisely to hold his back at the proper angle. An emperor of real estate has chairs like this.

Katzman waves away the distinction. "What's the difference if you play poker with plastic chips or silver dollars? It's the game that counts, am I right? You're a player or you're not."

"And I'm a player?" Segal says.

"Like me," Katzman says. "Not a crazy person, not a bum, not a pervert—this I can see. So why?"

Segal opens his mouth to speak; Katzman holds up a hand. "I don't want to hear that word."

"What else?" Segal says.

He regrets leaving the marvelous chair but he can see it's time to go home. He catches a glimpse of himself reflected in the stainless-steel side of the refrigerator: stylized down to form and color and movement, like a Kabuki character. The essential Segal. Katzman follows him through the living room. At the door they stop and shake hands. Katzman swings open the great oak panel and Segal steps through. It's past midnight and Sherman Oaks is quiet; the only thing Segal can hear is the sigh of the wind through Katzman's evergreens and, far away, the whisper of traffic on the Ventura Freeway. He's stepping down the driveway, watching where he puts his feet in the dark, when suddenly Katzman's floodlights go on like the noonday sun. Segal stops, frozen, his hand reaching for the Buick's door handle.

"Segal." The voice booms in the night. "Segal, you're not a bad person."

Segal shades his eyes but all he can see is the lights, haloed in purple, hurting his eyes. Katzman is in the shadows. "I'm trying to say: next Saturday night. Don't forget. She'll be here."

"Why?" Segal says.

"Love," Katzman shouts into the night that smells of evergreens, car exhaust, tropical flowers. "Why not? It's possible."

Segal backs the Buick down the rest of the driveway. At the bottom of the hill he swings onto the freeway. The radio plays something with hundreds of violins, the kind of sappy music he would never sell in his store. *Why not?* he thinks. He thinks *it could happen.*

Peacock Blue

When I was twelve years old and a good deal more certain about the world than I am now, my father bought me a used three-speed Raleigh bicycle; I took it down to the basement we shared with the Schades and painted it peacock blue.

Schade and his wife were very old now but they had managed to have two children late in life, in a final spurt of fertility before the good times passed forever. Georgia Schade, who later became my wife, was eleven; her brother Joseph, the last of the last, was nine. There had been another child, the product of the Schades' first flowering, but he had died tragically and discouraged them from trying again for a long time. Georgia told me that he'd drowned while sailing a model boat in a public fountain. The then-young Schades had turned to each other on their stone bench and lost themselves in a long kiss; by the time they came back to the world and remembered their child, little Jubal Schade had slipped, hit his head on the stone coping, and was floating irretrievably face down in the doubtful water.

Peacock blue is a color darker than sky, brighter than navy, somewhere this side of electric. I had wrapped the wheels of my bicycle in newspapers to keep paint off the spokes and tires; a picture of Toledo's mayor stared at me through the front fork, transfigured by drops of celestial blue. Summer had been a long time coming, but now, as I laid the paint over the bike's original shabby black, I could feel it at my fingers' ends; I almost had hold of it.

"I think that's going to look dumb," Georgia Schade said. She had come quietly down the basement stairs to stand behind me.

"What's dumb about it?" But I knew what she meant; I was laying on the paint like an amateur and I could tell it would never come smooth. It clung to the tube frame and to the arched fenders, clumsy, brilliant. I didn't care.

"Dumb," she repeated. She was an odd girl; she did things that made me uneasy. The top floor we rented from the Schades had no private entrance; the flight of stairs we took to get to our place passed through the center of the house and we walked by the Schades' closed doors to go home. From time to time, by what I believed then to be coincidence, Georgia would come out of the bathroom without any clothes on just as I was passing by. She squealed and wrapped her arms around herself, but I remember now that it took her a perceptible moment to step back inside the steamy bathroom every time.

"Yeah? Well I don't care—I like it," I said.

Banners of dusty sunlight fell from the high basement windows, cutting the gloom into uneven rectangles and making it darker. In front of us the coal furnace squatted cold and silent, holding up the house in its thick tube arms. My happiness that afternoon was just this side of being unendurable.

"I'm not allowed to wrestle with you any more," Georgia said.

I moved my brush slowly down the front fender; a small drop of blue fell in the mayor's right eye and gave him a shifty look. "All right," I said.

"You know why?"

"No."

"Because."

I stopped painting. "Because what?"

"I can't tell you."

"All right," I said.

"You'd have to promise never to tell anyone I told you."

"I promise," I said.

"It was my dad. He said it wasn't right for us to wrestle because I'm not a girl any more."

"What are you then?" I was puzzled.

"A woman," she said. Her voice took on mysterious harmonies when she said it, and her eyes glazed over as if she was looking at a religious object. The object turned out to be Georgia; a broken storm window leaning against the furnace reflected her image and she stared at herself with awe.

"First of all, that isn't true," I said. "You're only eleven years old. You're not even as old as I am."

"In India some eleven-year-old girls have babies," she said.

I pretended to dip my brush and wipe off the excess paint on the rim of the can, but I studied Georgia out of the corner of my eye. She was wearing a T-shirt, and indisputable breasts no larger than lemons lurked under the fabric, giving strength to her claim.

"Yeah, but this is Ohio; we're not in India," I said.

She turned away from me and favored the old furnace with a superior smile; she threw her shoulders back and stepped slowly through one of the bright banners of sun toward the basement stairs, as if to leave. But she stopped at the bottom and leaned on the banister; one breast just touched the painted wood of the railing.

I knew that at the age of twelve I wasn't nearly ready to be a father—if she could have babies, even if it was in India, it gave her an edge I would never overcome. "Why are you walking funny?" I said.

"My father said you probably wouldn't understand if I told you." she said. She tossed her hair, glancing at the storm window. "You're not to touch me in certain places any more, either."

"What?"

"When we play. If we play. I'm a woman now, and you have to treat me with respect."

That was the end of my perfect summer before it started, though it took me a while to notice the flaw. When the paint on my bicycle was dry I rode it around and around the little streets that wound back on themselves in self-conscious curves. I loved the machine already: the way a flick of my thumb could shift from one gear to the next, the long easy roll of the front wheel over the minor irregularities of the asphalt, most of all the glory of the peacock-blue paint on frame and fenders. But while I made my swoops and aimless circles all through our neighborhood, a piece of me was back in the basement; I kept seeing in my mind's eye Georgia Schade having babies in India, and her peculiar sashaying walk through the dusty slices of sun that fell through the windows crept into the rhythm of my pedaling.

My parents were serious people, a lot younger than the Schades but no less firm about what they expected from the world and what the world could expect from them—not in return but in the course of the natural sweetness and decorum of existence. My father taught tenth-through-twelfth-grade English and coached the football team at Perrysburg Country Day School; my mother was a secretary at the YMCA. At night she worked off part of our rent by typing for Schade, who relaxed from his university teaching by doing translations of Jules Verne. Among the sounds that mark that summer for me are the clatter of her old Royal, the chime at the end of each line, and the rustle of another clean page being fed into the roller.

Someday my parents planned to buy a house of their own, and probably they would rent the top floor to another young couple next in line for the serious life. I looked at them with mixed feelings: my dad in his chair underlining *Beowulf,* my mother leaning over to read Schade's difficult handwriting, and I saw that for them life was a progress, skirting pitfalls and avoiding temptations. My pilgrim parents.

Of the two it was my father who talked to me more, but we never stayed with it for more than half a dozen sentences at a time. Not that he was humorless, or lacked a feel for that deep absurdity at the bottom of it all, but he couldn't share it with me easily. One night I walked beside him to the corner drugstore to get cigarettes; on the way back he stopped under a streetlight.

"Women don't always understand," he said. He stood with the pack of Chesterfields in one hand, holding the red strip of cellophane between two fingers.

"Understand what?"

"What I mean is, they don't worry about the same things that men do." He tapped a cigarette out of the pack and lit it. "I'm going to quit," he said. "It's a bad habit. Suicide, if you keep at it." We walked along quietly for a while. It was a warm night and behind open windows people watched their televisions; we could see blue gleams in the dark houses, and hear bits and snatches of programs washed into the street.

"Hemingway had a lot of crazy ideas about the world," my father said. "And naturally there's the fact that he blew off the back of his own head with a shotgun—there isn't any way around that." He threw away the butt of his cigarette; it made a little twisting spark that arched into the gutter and died there. "Women don't like him much," he said. "But he wrote two or three books that you can still count on."

Just before we got to the house he stopped again. "Your mother doesn't like him at all," he said. I wanted to ask why that was important, but he had already told me as much as he could and he ran up the front steps to escape.

Which brings me to where I sit now, twenty-three years later, facing a window which faces a California freeway. I feel as hollow as a blown egg. In another house a thousand miles up the coast in Seattle my son is twelve years old and waits for me to say the words that might have made a difference that long-ago summer in Toledo if my father had found them to say to me. And following the family tradition I don't have anything better than faith in Hemingway to offer him. Two or three books he can count on. And admiration for a man who blew off the back of his own head with a shotgun, an act I have learned to think of as neither brave nor cowardly.

"Dear Thomas," I want to write. But I don't know what comes after that; my memory of my father jinxes me and I want to trot away from my son even in this letter. "How are you?" I end up saying. "What are you doing in school? Do you have any friends?"

I am seventy miles south of Los Angeles, stranded on

this cheaply magical coast, and the cars race by on the freeway in front of my window, toward San Diego and Tijuana, the beaches and the pretty restaurants of La Jolla. I have many friends but I can't stand to talk to the closest of them for more than twenty minutes before a deafening boredom sets in. Like my father I also have students, though mine are a little older, a little less well treated by the world. They come to Carlsbad Community College and I give them, for a gift, grammar and a belief in Standard English to help them along their pilgrim's way through the serious life.

My father packed his clothes one hot night in August twenty-two years ago and took a room over a drugstore in Perrysburg. My mother and I stayed at the Schades' house and every other weekend I visited my dad in his badly aired room with the brown floors. We sat at the kitchen table and played cribbage, he cooked hamburgers on a two-burner gas range, and we hardly ever talked at all. When I got home early Sunday nights my mother would look up from *De la Terre a la Lune*, Englished in violet ink in Schade's tiny handwriting, and ask me how he was. Our talk about my parents' separation didn't go beyond that.

I have faith in the vigorous life and I run my three miles on the beach every day unless the weather is bad; it hardly ever is. Jets and helicopters from the El Toro Naval Air Station swoop low over me while I jog, and back in the yellow hills the boys from Camp Pendleton practice with their howitzers and mortars. The distant explosions sound like the paper bags I blew into and broke when I was a kid. Their noise makes me feel better. The tourists make me feel better, and so does the far-off rumble of freight trains at night. Even the

smog that comes down on us when the Santa Ana
winds blow in Los Angeles is a sign that people up
there still have an interest in making things that smoke
and smell bad.

After my run I go to school and dance through the
halls with my students, my colleagues, an occasional
dean caught in the rush between classes.

"Dear Thomas," I repeat in my mind while my students bend their heads over examples of clumsy sentences and try to figure out where they went wrong.
"Dear Thomas, I would like to explain to you about
life, but I don't know very much about it and probably
never will. Find your own way without advice from
Your Loving Father."

My second run of the day. The flap-flap of my bare
feet on the damp sand awakens some of the near-dead
dozing on the slight slope to the sea, and they raise
their heads to see a youngish man trotting steadily
south along the edge of the tide, where the water has
retreated, leaving a fringe of sea-sputum, foam, and
broken shells.

That September after a flawed summer spent thinking about Georgia Schade, I went back to Perrysburg
Country Day School, where my father's position on the
faculty entitled me to a place among the sons of Jeep
executives, real-estate men, and tool-and-die tycoons.
In the long fragrant fall afternoons I worked out with
the junior high team and listened to my dad, on the
next field, putting the older boys through their paces.
He didn't have much to work with; there were twenty-
six boys in the senior high, of whom two were cripples
and one a resolute intellectual, leaving my old man
with twenty-three bodies. But he faced each new sea-

son with confidence; he was a believer in strategies, and devised fantastic formations and trick plays to make up for the lack of manpower. During football season his table talk was full of two-eight-one defenses and unbalanced lines. His tackles were often eligible and his guards dreamed of taking the snap from center and running to glory while the quarterback zigzagged in the backfield to lull the defense.

In October Perrysburg won its second football game in three years and my father blew himself up with his two-burner gas range, possibly on purpose. It happened early in the morning. I rode my blue bicycle to school; before I could get it parked I noticed my friends gathering around to stare at me with serious, peculiar faces. The assistant principal, Mr. Rodeheaver, cut through the circle and put his arm around my shoulder. I helped him load the bike into the trunk of his car, where the paint left long blue streaks on the carpeting, and he drove me home. Old Mrs. Schade was hugging my mother; Mr. Schade, Georgia, and Joseph stood in the dark hall wearing expressions of fascinated gloom, like spectators at a car accident.

Later that afternoon, having learned from my mother how he died, I took a bus to where my dad had lived. The city hadn't had time to clean up very much; his room fronted the street and the power of the explosion had knocked the wall straight outward. Bricks lay in a heap across the sidewalk, full of shiny fragments of window glass; long strips of wallpaper blew from the opening on the second floor like party decorations; a piece of brown linoleum hung down over the drugstore's miraculously undamaged plate-glass window like a dirty dead tongue.

A pretty girl in a red swimsuit comes out of the waves and stops, up to her knees in the roiling water, to stare at me. I smile back and without my willing it at all my stride lengthens, my shoulders square themselves, and something in my head goes to work calculating chances I don't want to take.

Georgia, my wife, writes that Thomas is doing as well as can be expected from a kid with no father. She signed up a University of Washington fraternity man to be his Big Brother, and she tells me in every letter where they went camping together, how this rich man's kid from Delta Kappa Upsilon took my son to the zoo, to the circus, to the rodeo, where a fallen rider was nearly kicked to death by a bull. How did the fraternity man cope with that? I wonder. How did he explain to a twelve-year-old that we all have to bleed?

She is only a year younger than I am, but I think sometimes she has not learned a damn thing since that June afternoon in the Schades' basement when she decided, with her father's word for it, that she was a woman. I have news for her this evening from California: she wasn't a woman then and she isn't now, though we had our child without going to India and her breasts got to be big and she let me hold them when we made love.

A year after my father died my mother and I moved to New York and I lost track of Georgia. We met again by chance at a miserably dull party in Manhattan; we went for a walk, thought we fell in love, got married in good faith, and learned to dislike each other.

I jog down the long stretch of sand, thinking what lucky fools marathon runners are. They run for joy. I run to ease myself out of life and some days I do my three miles before school, again after dinner, and if I can't sleep I get out of bed to come here and run a third time, under the yellow moon. *De la Terre a la Lune:* my mother finished the typing that winter by way of something to do and because she wasn't certain

that the insurance company would call my dad's death
an accident and pay off his policy. I proofread for her
and I remember Jules Verne's characters sailing in
their aluminum bullet around this moon, high on pure
oxygen, anticipating the twentieth century.

I get to running faster and faster until I'm charging
down the silent beach, arms pumping, legs flailing. I'm
going as fast as a bicycle, faster. A cloud crosses the sun
and shadows the water and I feel myself beginning to
cry, though I'm not particularly sad. The sea under the
cloud is a peculiar lucid blue, deeper than sky, somewhere this side of electric.

Diehl: The Wandering Years

In the end Diehl went back to Santa Barbara. He drove the Datsun up the coast highway from Oceanside, through Los Angeles, Ventura, and Oxnard; he listened to the radio and watched the surfers in their black suits, bobbing in the water, waiting for *the* wave. It was late February and Diehl planned to be gone from California before the calendar rolled into March. He visualized it like an old movie cut: the little square pages of days fluttering and tearing themselves away, blown out of the picture. Out beyond the surfers he could see the drilling platforms standing in the Channel, spraddle-legged, sucking at the bottom. Three years ago, when he had lived in Santa Barbara with Anna, he had hated both the platforms and the surfers; now he didn't give a damn.

Before going up to Flaherty's house, Diehl sat under the big fig tree on Anacapa Street. It had been one of his favorite places; he'd come to it nearly every afternoon, wrung out from writing for four or five hours straight. Flaherty and that tree had held Diehl together for two years, while his wife had left and come back and left again for good, and while he had tried to write his second novel, in which he was going to avoid all the mistakes of the first. Flaherty was the one sane man Diehl knew. In a world falling to pieces Flaherty was a rock. He never talked about himself in class, but Diehl knew from the other students that he'd lost his son in Vietnam, had his left hand torn off in a car accident, had written a book about Matthew Arnold.

In those days when the new novel was first getting under way, Diehl had loved his central character, maybe because Chalumeau's troubles were greater than his own. Then as Anna got crazier and crazier it became harder for Diehl to feel sorry for Chalumeau in his cool comfortable hole. By then it was summer and an abnormal heat wave was blasting Santa Barbara. Diehl was too poor to buy an air-conditioner and by midmorning he'd be sitting stark naked at the typewriter. Anna was disgusted with him.

Out of love with his hero, he'd gradually stopped writing, though he went on sitting in front of the machine, a towel draped over the back of the chair to soak up the sweat.

"Why don't you quit?" Anna asked him after a month of inaction.

"Dumb bitch," Diehl muttered. "What do you know about writing?"

"I know when somebody's not doing it," she told him.

He went to see Flaherty in his house up on the mesa. "I'm over thirty," he moaned, clutching a beer, looking at Joan Flaherty cool in a tennis dress. "I'm going to die."

"Novel not going so well?" Flaherty said.

"I can't afford to make any mistakes," Diehl explained.

By then he hadn't typed a word he could keep in more than two months, and he found himself taking a sly pleasure in his wife's sarcasm, thinking *dumb bitch,* thinking *I deserve it.* More than once he was tempted to pull the pages he *had* written out of their box and burn them in front of her to show her he cared. It had taken him six weeks of nervous mornings fingering the Selectric to get Chalumeau in the ground, and then he had bogged down completely. He sat after breakfast every day, tapping the keys, hoping for character and conflict and plot and higher meaning to emerge from the little jumping golf ball.

Chalumeau lived in Forest Hills; he had buried himself in his front yard in a last-ditch effort to understand life. Chalumeau was a wholesale plumber and owned a big house south of Queens Boulevard; he dug his grave in the lawn, under a Norwegian spruce, a hole six feet deep by three feet by six feet long. He cut pine planks on the table saw in his garage, glued and screwed them together into a reasonable coffin. He lined his box with a quilt, put in a pillow from his bed, a five-gallon water can with a long tube for sucking, a bedpan. He made a vent long enough to reach the surface out of a piece of two-inch plastic pipe. He lowered the coffin in the hole at night, pulled the lid over himself, and had his wife shovel the earth back on top of him. He ordered her to replace the turf just as it had been; he had no desire to startle the neighbors. He gave himself a week, and asked his wife not to come speak to him unless she had to, and then only at night, when people wouldn't see her bending down to speak into the pipe sticking out of the ground.

She came the next day. "How can you do this to me?" she hissed.

Given the circumstances a great deal of the opening section of the book had to be given to Chalumeau's thoughts—there was no room in the box for action. He could turn on his side; he could wriggle himself into position to use the bedpan; he could bend one leg at a time, and very little else. Any action would have had to be a flashback (Diehl wanted to preserve point of view) and he thought he'd used too many flashbacks and played too many games with the steady run of time in the first book. This story was going to be strictly straightforward, a realistic novel in the narrowest sense.

Diehl got up from under the fig tree and walked slowly across the railroad tracks, down to the harbor, and out on the pier. He stood for a long time looking into the salt-water tanks where the crabs huddled by the dozens, slowly scraping over each other. He hadn't eaten since early in the morning in Oceanside and he considered buying a crab and having it boiled, but he decided not to. When he was in a dark mood Diehl didn't like to think about anything dying to feed him. All dying reminded him of his own. The worse the melancholy the more Diehl inclined to vegetables and fruits and clear water.

For a while he watched three old men in canvas chairs trailing long lines over the railing into the sea. Diehl, who had lived two blocks from the harbor, had never actually seen anyone catch a fish off the pier, but the old men were always there.

It was time to go see Flaherty; he turned back to look for his car. When he passed his old apartment, a kid waved at him from what had been his and Anna's living room window; on the other side of that flat glass Diehl had sat naked in front of his typewriter, listening to Anna curse him and bang the dishes around in the sink. The sky above Santa Barbara today was a flat wash of blue, the palm trees stood against it like cheerful green and brown paper cutouts.

With Anna gone for good, Diehl had wandered, and

he had begun to write again, but he hadn't been able to make it stick. After all this time Chalumeau still lay under the green grass of home, waiting for his author to resurrect him. His wife was still where we last saw her, bent over the pipe, whispering accusations into what she assumed was her husband's ear.

Diehl had raised him a dozen times in a dozen different cities, always in vain. He had a cardboard box full of the rejected pages; he lugged it with him everywhere and never looked into it. Sometimes, if the apartment he found was insufficiently furnished, he used the box as a table for the Selectric. Diehl had learned to type on a coffee table and always felt most comfortable with the machine below him, at his fingers' ends, where he could look into the works and watch the golf ball bounce, making words. Wasted words, for the past months, years.

He had stamina, and he had fear to keep him going. Several times already he'd taken the book clear to its end—various ends for various towns. In Phoenix he'd drowned Chalumeau in the East River, fallen from the ferry. In Tucson in summer Diehl sweated worse than he had in Santa Barbara and Chalumeau rose from the grave and joined the Mafia; he was rubbed out in a gang war in the Bronx. In El Paso, city of light, Diehl made Chalumeau an underground man. He rode the subways and refused to come up; he slept on the trains, showered in the men's rooms of Pennsylvania Station, ate his meals in underground restaurants. In this version he remained a wholesale plumber; he made his deals by telephone, lugged his catalogues, carried his office in his briefcase. He zoomed without end from Flushing to Far Rockaway, Harlem to Brooklyn Heights. That story too, Diehl rejected. He liked it the best, but who would have believed it? Not even Diehl.

In Boston Diehl shivered in a Roxbury cold-water flat and thought up a Chalumeau who came out of the coffin and resumed his previous life; but something had triggered a Bacchus in him and he spent his after-work hours chasing every young girl between Continental Avenue and Yellowstone Boulevard. No babysitter, no cheerleader, no short-skirted innocent bringing home bread and milk from the market was safe from Chalumeau. Winter finally pushed Diehl into a corner and he left Boston for Albuquerque, Albuquerque for Denver, where Chalumeau went back to the grave and rose from the dead again.

Through his travels Diehl kept the same car he started with, a Datsun bought new with the money from the first novel. By now it was scraped on all sides, rusty and bent; the seats were ripped and sagging; the headliner hung in strips. It was an eyesore, but it still ran sweet as long as Diehl remembered to put in new plugs and change the oil. In the back seat were hundreds of copies of Diehl's first book, which he had bought before it was remaindered. They were what he could see in the mirror when he drove the interstates; stacked to the roof they made the little car sit cockeyed, wore out Diehl's back tires, made his steering light and uncertain.

A letter from Flaherty found him in Seattle, where he had started fresh again; Chalumeau had popped out of the earth, puzzled by waking dreams, looking for wisdom. Flaherty was dying. Diehl jumped back into the Datsun and raced down the long valleys to California to see his old teacher, his friend. But when he hit the city limits of Santa Barbara he kept on going, struck with sudden indecision. He wound up in Oceanside, a little north of San Diego. There he stayed until February; he sent Chalumeau to see priests, ministers, rabbis. He made friends with a writer who didn't throw his work away; he walked the warm beaches at night; he found a girl he liked. Finally he packed up again and headed north to see Flaherty.

Joan Flaherty met him at the door. Flaherty's wife had always impressed the hell out of Diehl. She was his second wife, much younger than her husband, a tall thin woman, precise and graceful in her movements. Diehl was afraid that she understood him too well. He was convinced that someday she would say, "Diehl, let me tell you what's wrong with you." And she'd be right on the mark.

"You took your time," she said.

"Troubles on the road."

"For three months?"

"Is he all right?" Diehl said.

"He's been worrying about you."

Through the French doors he could see Flaherty out on the patio, his back to them, staring out over the Channel. Beyond the blue water Diehl could barely make out the shadow of the islands.

"There isn't much pain yet," she said. "We don't know when it'll start. Go on out, he's waiting for you."

Diehl pushed open the doors and walked around the chairs to take Flaherty's good right hand; the left, a complicated mechanical claw in chromed steel, rested on the table, hooked around a pencil.

The hand Diehl held was light and fragile. He thought he could feel it tremble, but he was nervous, maybe he was feeling himself shake. "I'm going great guns," Flaherty said. The claw tapped a pile of yellow paper. "Poems about childhood—I'm trying to put a collection together. And you?"

"I keep moving," Diehl said.

Flaherty looked at him seriously. "That's what I hear. What about the novel?"

"Out of control," Diehl said. A boat in the Channel hooted; in the house above Flaherty's somebody was playing Bach very loud on the stereo. The master's intricate certainties made Diehl feel like a clumsy fool, a ditherer.

"What are you going to do next?" Flaherty said.

Instead of answering, Diehl studied the long complicated fall of the hill down to the harbor; the ground took a steep drop to another street, rebounded, dropped again, and slipped down to the sea. The slope was covered with trees and gaudy flowering shrubs and Diehl had to look twice to see the houses. In the harbor small boats sailed zigzag, contradictory courses; way to the south an outfall of red and brown smoke into the sea announced Los Angeles.

"I thought maybe I'd go to Montana. I've never been there except to drive through."

"What for?" Flaherty said.

"To finish the book, maybe. I don't know."

He lay awake all night in their guest room. A hard-edged full moon came down the skylight and used itself against the redwood walls. The bed was wide and soft and Diehl thought of Chalumeau, locked up between wooden walls in a narrower context, with his wife's accusing voice falling on his ear. "Why are you doing this to me?"

He hadn't realized until this moment that he had been quoting Anna word for word. Women take everything personally, he thought. He stared up and out at the mountains of the moon.

In the morning Flaherty told him he should stay. Diehl shook his head. "I don't think it's a good idea."

"There's a desk in the room," Joan Flaherty said. "Or you could work out here if you wanted."

Flaherty lifted his arm; the claw flashed in the sun like a knife. "You don't have to make up your mind right now."

"We'd love to have you," Joan said.

Diehl felt morose, unloved and unlovable. He had stared at the cold lunar landscape until the disk had slipped out of the skylight's frame, and he had felt himself drawn after it. He couldn't sleep. The moon looked like a skull. He spent the rest of the night wondering what it was going to be like to die. To dwindle to a speck of consciousness and disappear.

Non-being—that was what frightened Diehl. Even though, as the Greeks had pointed out, he wouldn't be there to see it. How could there still be a world, and Diehl not be? he asked himself. He knew the answer.

"I could pay some rent," he told Flaherty.

Every day at ten o'clock Flaherty went off to his office at the university. He seemed able to drive the station wagon with easy skill despite the missing hand. Joan ignored Diehl, leaving him carefully to his own devices, to write or not, as he pleased. Writing, he decided the first morning, is sometimes a way of avoiding coming to terms with a book. For a week he had enough strength of character to leave the typewriter unplugged. He went for long foolish walks, came back to sit in the room and stare at the stacked boxes of his first book. TELL HIM I WAS FLYING, a novel by L. D. Diehl. And beside that a smaller box with enough typed pages in it to make up several novels, but which added up to damn-all. Poor Chalumeau was a-mouldering in the grave and looked likely to stay that way. In the meantime Flaherty, the only really sane person Diehl knew, was going to die. Diehl wanted to be long gone and far away when it happened.

For now he stayed and tried to discipline himself not to write. He ate cabbage, lettuce, carrots, avocados, spinach, green beans, corn. He watched Flaherty for signs of the end. He suffered from excessive wind and often felt tired. He craved meat but didn't dream of eating it. He fell in love with Flaherty's wife.

It was less of a surprise to her than it was to Diehl; she'd been watching him mope around the house, come back from his walks with a lost expression on his face, stare moonstruck at the distant shadows of the Channel Islands across the water, and she noticed it before he did when his eyes began to follow her instead of the landscape.

"I'm sorry," Diehl said.

"It's natural," she told him.

"I'll have to leave."

"We're both grown-up," she said. Diehl, she implied, would restrain himself.

He made his walks longer; he read modern poetry from Flaherty's bookshelves, did pushups, sat in the bushes just off the patio where he could secretly watch her. He called himself hard names.

He went down to the harbor and tried to talk to the old men on the pier, but they didn't want anything to do with him—they could smell a bad man, Diehl thought. He stood half an hour at a time watching the slow movements of the crabs in their rusty tank as they looked for a way out.

He plugged in the Selectric and went back with a sense of relief to Chalumeau's problems, more tolerable than his own. He began again with his wife's whisper. "Why are you doing this to me?"

"Women take things too personally," Chalumeau whispered back. "This is between me and God. Go to bed. Read a good book. Watch the midnight movie. Leave me alone."

"You bastard," she whispered back down the pipe.

She was only seven feet away but her voice seemed to Chalumeau to be coming from another world. "You won't get away with this," she hissed.

Why not? Diehl wondered. The little plumber was invulnerable in his hole. Down there he could get away with anything—everything was allowed. He looked at his watch and found he'd been sitting in front of the typewriter for hours—it was after three o'clock in the morning. He looked up at the skylight, hoping for a moon, but clouds had blown in from the west and all Diehl saw was undifferentiated darkness.

He turned when he heard the door open. "Hello," Joan Flaherty said.

"How's it going?" Diehl said. He forgot that his fingers were resting on the keys and the machine suddenly typed half a line of nonsense before he thought to lift his hands. He ripped the page out and wadded it up. "What do you want?"

"I'm sorry," she said. She stayed in the doorway, looking down at Diehl. He was sitting on the edge of his bed; he had pulled the redwood burl coffee table over and set up the machine on it. He put in a new page, began to type from memory. Chalumeau, he suddenly realized, was a dead man. All his careers were dreams—he was down there to stay.

"What are you going to do?" Chalumeau asked his wife. But no words came down the pipe. "Hello?" Nothing. He called again. "Hello?"

Dreams. Diehl saw it clearly. All those versions had been right. He had written his book without knowing it. He had himself a novel. Chalumeau the Mafioso; Chalumeau on the subways of New York; Chalumeau the lecher; Chalumeau with the scholars and the rabbis. Nothing but visions from underground.

"Hello up there," Chalumeau called out. His mouth

was dry; he sucked up some stale water through the tube. "Hello?"

The first few grains of earth that fell on his cheek he thought were a mistake—a faulty joint somewhere—but the rush that followed left no room for doubt. His wife was trying to bury him for good. He even made out the tap of her shovel against the edge of the pipe as she prepared to pour another load down. Quickly he turned himself on his back and clapped the palm of his hand to the opening. How long could he hold off the dirt? Until she got tired, he decided. All she could do was fill up the pipe; when she gave it up and went to bed he'd let it empty itself into the box and he'd be open to the world of breathers again. Lucky for him he'd been neglecting the yard; the dirt was loose and sandy and would fall easily.

"You're busy," Joan said. Diehl hardly looked up.

Chalumeau felt a strong pulsing of the earth against his palm; he realized that she must be using the handle of the shovel to tamp the dirt. But there was too much friction in the system and she had never been a strong woman. No more than a handful of fine dust spilled past his palm.

"You're very intense when you're writing," Joan said.

"Don't talk to me now," Diehl begged her.

The pounding from above stopped and Chalumeau relaxed. She had given up more easily than he'd expected. Then he remembered that she had to go to the garage to get the shovel, and remembered the nine-foot-long iron digging bar he kept behind the door. He didn't think she'd have the strength to lift it high enough to clear the mouth of the pipe. He heard her footsteps, a faint dull vibration in the earth, coming back. He imagined her setting herself solidly, using all her strength to raise the bar. He made himself small against one side of the box, took his hand from the pipe. Dirt rolled out, nearly choked him. When nothing happened he decided he had misjudged her.

Something shot down the pipe, bringing with it another fall of earth; the bar hit the bottom of the box with a tremendous blow and went on through. If Chalumeau had stayed where he was he would have been staked through the heart like a vampire. His wife began to pull the bar back up, but Chalumeau, always a quick thinker, quicker than ever now, grabbed the iron with both hands. He had the advantage of weight and leverage and desperation, and after several ineffective yanks she gave up.

The dirt in his eyes made him weep; he coughed, sneezed, inhaled more dirt, nearly strangled, kept his grip on the iron bar. The upper world was silent. Chalumeau waited as long as he could stand it, then let go long enough to wipe his eyes.

"I love you," Flaherty's wife said to Diehl.

I love you, Diehl typed. "I love you," Chalumeau's wife whispered down the pipe. "Please don't be dead. I'm sorry. I'm sorry. Please."

Chalumeau sneezed again. "Go to hell," he cried. His voice was choked and terrible with all the dirt he'd swallowed.

"I was crazy," she said. "Forgive me. I miss you. I can't sleep if you're not there. I love you. Forgive me."

"All right," Chalumeau said. He eased himself into a more comfortable position. "Maybe it's been my fault too. Who's perfect?"

"Not me," Joan Flaherty said. Diehl was startled at the sound.

"Did you know you talk out loud when you're writing?" she said.

"Anna used to complain," Diehl said.

"Do you miss her?"

"Never."

What he did miss was being married. Living alone had obvious advantages but it was too loose a life to suit Diehl completely. Someday he'd live with somebody again. Maybe when the book was done.

Joan stood up and stretched. She had on a thin peach-colored night dress and Diehl could see the shape of her breasts and farther down a dark shadow he wanted to kiss. She had wonderful legs. Flaherty was dying.

"I really liked your first book," she said.

It irritated him to hear anyone praise it now. "I don't like to talk about it any more."

Joan leaned forward and kissed him on the cheek. "This isn't the right time, is it?" she said. "I feel like I'm going to be ignored."

"I have to work now," Diehl said. He started reading the page caught in the Selectric. Behind him the door opened and closed, a repressed slam.

It remained only to get Chalumeau out of his hole, or else to have his treacherous wife do him in after all. Either way, it was going to be the end of the book. The lives Chalumeau had lived in his mind would be the bulk of the novel; those dream lives were the treasure he went underground to find, only the dragon ate him. Maybe. That was the only open question, really: whether he was coming back alive from the expedition. Diehl, sitting at his machine, couldn't decide. The vision of these more than middle-aged lovers whispering their renewed affection up and down that short length of pipe which crossed an unnameable gulf, fascinated him. But there was a satisfying finality to be earned by killing the plumber.

When day came he still hadn't made up his mind. He

undressed, showered, whistled the three or four tunes he knew while he soaped himself. He was pleased with the underground echo off the tiles. He dressed in clean clothes and went out the back door, down a long flight of narrow wooden stairs to the street below, hoping no one would see him leave. He walked all the way to the harbor.

Someone had anchored a Chinese junk inside the breakwater. False or real—Diehl couldn't tell the difference. He stared at the painted woodwork and the slatted sails. The fake and the real were equally likely here, just ninety miles north of Hollywood. Even from where he stood Diehl could tell that the ship looked as if it had been built in a hurry by people who didn't care, but he didn't know if that meant anything. For all he knew the Chinese were sloppy builders too.

The three old men at the end of the pier were only two this morning; there was an empty canvas chair between them. Diehl was afraid to ask why.

"Should have been here twenty minutes ago," one of them said. "Samuel caught the biggest yellowtail you ever saw."

"Where?" Diehl said.

"Right here off the pier."

"I mean where's the fish?"

"He took it over on State Street to see if one of them restaurants would give him anything for it. At our age we don't eat much."

So they did catch fish here, Diehl thought. But the old men looked sly and he suspected it might be just another story. He knew that kids sometimes bought whole fish from the boats and pretended to hook them off the pier so they could sell them to watching tourists for double what they'd paid.

He strolled back to the crab tanks and looked inside.

He was hungry. He thought about Chalumeau flat on his back in his wooden box, talking to his fifty-year-old wife about love. What the hell, he thought. He signaled the crab man, bought one, had it boiled, ate it with satisfaction. He sucked the meat out of a leg, stared out at the sea. He decided Chalumeau didn't have to die. He finished his crab and walked back to the tank again.

"I'll have another one," he said "That one there in the corner. The one with the big blue eyes."

A Special Case

Harry Caudill studied his naked self in the mirror. He had imperceptibly turned into a fat man. A fat man in a strange place, he thought; he felt Ohio all about him, surrounding the cottage he rented from Marvella, pressing on the walls. A wooden clacking from the weather vane on the roof signaled a shift in the Ohio wind. Being away from home made him feel out of sorts; even after nearly six months at Goshen College as poet-in-residence he was still having trouble reconciling himself to this place. It was the winding roads, the trees and grass everywhere, the dark fertility of the manured soil that made him uneasy; he missed the string-straight highways, the arid fields of Kansas.

But this morning's quirky depression came from somewhere else in his head. Did it have to do with love? He looked at himself in the mirror. Who could love me? He didn't care. Three wives had left him, and each time after an initial keen sense of loss he had been more relieved than depressed. The last one had fled his house in Wichita nearly eight years before, and since then Harry had reconciled himself to going it alone.

He finished drying himself with one of the deep pink towels that Marvella provided, and dropped it on

the bathroom floor. Marvella loved poets and professors and did her best to make them happy; so far he
had been able to avoid her.

He patted his stomach and decided that the extra
bulk suited his years. It made him stand out among the
thin students, gave him dignity. Nonetheless a vague
dissatisfaction with himself had settled over him this
morning as congruently as a second skin. "Harry Caudill," he said out loud. He repeated his name, an incan-
tation, a spell against nameless devils. *Harry Caudill is
disappointed in life.* But that wasn't it. While he brushed
his teeth he tried to fit a word to the feeling and failed.
Anomie? No. He opened his mouth wide to the mirror
and leaned closer to see more clearly. Forty-nine years
old in three days and still with his own teeth; yellow
and tough, they were probably good for another forty-
nine years.

On the way to school he walked under trees that
grew too close together to seem completely natural;
they closed him off from the sky. A distant rumble of
thunder, felt more than heard, disturbed the air. A
random gust of wind shook the new leaves and Harry
looked up at the sound, thinking the rain had already
begun.

If it isn't love that's making me feel bad, he thought,
then it must be work. Between those two poles lie nine-
tenths of the man. But poems came when they wanted
to come. He'd stopped worrying about it a long time
ago. Sometimes he went six months without writing
one worth keeping; other times three or four came in
the same week. And he knew he wasn't going to be
Dylan Thomas. He was used to that too. No cause
there for that itchy dissatisfaction that clung to him
closer than cobwebs.

He stopped to let a girl in a long blue coat cross the
path. "Hi, Dr. Caudill." She had a model's narrow face,

with hollow cheeks and prominent bones. "Have a nice day," she said.

"Melancholia?" Harry said. The girl looked puzzled, but he was already gone.

During his classes Harry often found himself talking to one student only, somebody who singled himself out by chance at the start of the period. This morning it was a girl with gray eyes who sat all the way at the back of the room.

"We're all alone," Harry told her. "We're all going to die. It's a testimonial to the human spirit that we're not all down on that carpet writhing around and moaning at the idea."

The rain began to fall just before the final bell and he stepped outside as soon as he could shake off his students. He wanted to stand under the water; he hoped it would wash off his ill humor. But it turned out to be a drizzly and feckless Ohio rain, a mockery of the flailing storms that lashed the ground back home and made the dust fly.

"Damn," Harry said. "Oh damn!"

The girl from the back of the room had quietly come to stand beside him. "Excuse me?" she said.

"Not you," he explained. "The weather."

"You don't like rain?"

"I love it. This isn't rain."

"Oh," the girl said. She looked at him with interest. "Can I ask you a personal question?"

"What?"

"Why are you sad all the time?"

She had a sharp nose, a strong upper lip, brown hair brushed back behind her ears. When she smiled her teeth were white and blunt, outward sign of a kindly nature. "My name's Jo-Lynn," she told Harry.

"What do you mean, sad?" he said.

"You're always talking about dying and pain. What does that have to do with poetry?"

"Everything," Harry said. "Would you like to come have lunch with me?"

There must have been something showing in his face; she looked at him carefully, measuring.

"Just lunch," he said.

He was still explaining it to her and to himself when she climbed out of his bed a little before daylight. "I never do this," he swore.

"Hand me the panties," she said. "You don't have to apologize; you're a nice man. I understand what you mean."

"Sex doesn't solve anything."

She grinned and lifted her sharp nose. "That's not what you said five minutes ago." She turned to look at herself in Harry's bedroom mirror. "I like you."

"I'm getting old," he said.

She turned slowly in front of her reflection, hands held out from her sides. "Do you think my breasts are pretty?"

"Very beautiful," Harry said.

Through the window he could see all the way across the valley to the dark outline of the Welsh Hills, barely visible against a slightly less dark sky. Two or three points of light on the slopes looked like holes in a black swatch of fabric. "Farmers," Harry said. Jo-Lynn leaned down and kissed him on the mouth. He heard her start her car, pause at the end of the driveway, and accelerate up the hill. "They get up early," he said out loud. The weather vane clacked once. He felt a sharp sense of loss.

His third wife had fled to Boston; she was a Connecticut Quaker who had never adapted to Kansas. "They're all named Perry and they live in the back of campers," she had told the dean of liberal arts one evening when he asked her how she liked living in Wichita. Civilized Boston was an hour closer to morning than Ohio; she came to the phone wide awake.

"What happened to us?" Harry said. "I can't remember."

"You're feeling sorry for yourself," she said.

"How can you tell?"

"I bet you're fat by now. Are you a jolly fat man, Harry?"

"No," he lied. Half a lie—jolly he wasn't. "Say something nice to me, Laura," he begged.

"Like what?"

"Anything, goddamn it."

"If you're going to swear, I'll hang up, Harry."

"I'm beginning to remember," he said.

She waited. That was her strength, an uncanny ability to say nothing. Harry had watched her at faculty parties; she let articulate assistant professors beat themselves to death against the rock of her silences. He tried to wait her out; from the infinite spaces through which the telephone connection passed, a faint hiss fell into his ear. She didn't even seem to need to breathe. "Jesus!" he said finally. "All right. All right!"

Her laugh was without malice. "I didn't know anything when I married you," she said. "I thought you were a great man in the making; I was sure you were going to be a famous American poet and they'd write about me in your biography. I wanted to be your Nora Barnacle. But you're no Joyce, are you, Harry?"

"No."

"Well I don't hold a grudge. I mean after all it's not your fault, is it? You always worked at it as hard as you could. I personally hope you have lots of luck in life, Harry."

"Are we telling truths?" he said. "All right. You were a rotten cook and you couldn't be bothered to keep house and you weren't even that good-looking. About all you could do was fuck, and even there, you know, you weren't the thrill of a lifetime."

"My old Harry," she said. "So why did you stay married to me for three years and cry when I left?"

"I'm sentimental," he said.

As he listened to her it suddenly seemed to Harry that he was ceasing to breathe properly. He sucked in a great chestful of the night air but nothing reached the bottom of his lungs where he needed it the most. Fear wrapped itself around his chest like a wide leather strap tightened by a maniac. He told himself that it was psychological and would pass. At the other end of the line Laura was being silent again; Harry was unable to break through the strangler's grip to speak. The faint hiss he imagined originated in outer space tickled his inner ear. Finally she gave up and spoke first; he thought he heard respect in her tone.

"You're a son of a bitch, Harry," she said. "I remember that much."

As soon as he put down the phone the strap around his chest eased a notch; he stepped outside in his underwear for the sake of a little air, trusting to darkness to hide him from his neighbors.

Harry sat in his back yard at a card table, hacking and cutting at an old poem. Rooted in a Sunday afternoon in Kansas with his second wife, it now sprawled in ragged confusion over three pages of yellow legal pad. The sky above him was deeply, perfectly blue; white compact clouds shaped like puffballs voyaged slowly across it. With regret, Harry pruned a phrase. The fir tree above the table jiggled in the light wind; it let fall a shower of dry needles. Harry brushed them off the yellow page with his hand. He got ready to obliterate another word, changed his mind, pondered, changed it again and cut through a whole line with one stroke of the pen. When the doorbell rang, releasing him from the poem, he was grateful.

"You ought to be run out of town," the kid said.

"Who are you?" Harry asked him.

"You ought to be shot like a dog." The voice was high and nasal; it reminded Harry of the backcountry students in Kansas, who sometimes came to his classes and stared at him with suspicion from the farthest rows for a week or two before they disappeared.

"You ought to lose your job," the boy said. The twangy voice was beginning to whine like a loosening guitar string.

"Come inside," Harry told him.

The boy sat on the edge of Marvella's sofa and stared at the floor; his thin face was full of woe.

"Would you like a beer?"

"I don't drink."

"Coffee?"

"No." The boy looked up. "Jo-Lynn's a wonderful girl," he said. His hands knotted and unknotted themselves in his lap. He had enormous knuckles.

"Oh," Harry said. "I only saw her once, you know. Did she tell you that?"

"How can you sit there and talk about it?" the boy said. "It's bad enough knowing that you and Jo-Lynn . . ."

"Slept together?" Harry said.

"Oh God!" He hid his hands in his armpits and did a little stationary dance of despair, hugging himself and swaying from side to side. "What am I going to do?"

"Women are just like you and me," Harry said.

"They have urges. Whims. It didn't amount to anything."

The boy's face twisted. "That's sick," he said. He stared at Harry. His voice recovered some of its early fiber. "Jo-Lynn is like a goddess; she's wonderful and pure."

"Pure?" Harry said.

"A saint," the boy said. He broke into a strange giggle. "My folks would die if they heard me say that. I wasn't brought up to believe in saints. But that's what she is."

When he left, Harry found that the poem had agonized and died in his absence. He reread a stanza, tasted bile, and turned his head to spit. He looked up at the fir tree, and the long twigs waving slowly in the wind reminded him of the legs of venomous spiders; a puffball cloud crossed the innocent perfect sky and Harry saw foul vapors floating in an absurd illusion of blue that hid dark frightening spaces.

In two days, he thought, watching the tree and the cloud, I'm going to turn forty-nine. I've used up almost five-sevenths of my life, he calculated. My teeth will outlast me.

His second wife had stayed in Wichita; she was a local girl, a rancher's daughter with literary tastes. He imagined how this night must smell outside her window—dry and dusty, wonderful.

"Do you remember those Sunday afternoons when we used to put the top down on the Ford and drive out into the country with a two-dollar bottle of California champagne and some cold chicken?" he asked her.

"You have no idea how I hated those afternoons," she said.

Harry was hurt. "I used to call you Zelda and you

called me Scott and we'd read poetry to each other
under a tree, when we found a tree. You never told me
you hated it."

"I knew you liked it so much," she said. "But I always
thought it was a hell of a way to spend a Sunday."

"Anyway, how's your new husband?" he said. He'd
been on the verge of telling her about the poem, but
he saw it was a bad idea. Like his memory of those
days, the poem was false and useless.

"John and I've been married nearly five years—he's
hardly new. You don't have any sense of time passing
unless it's because something is happening to you,
Harry."

"Anyway . . ." he said.

"John and I are getting along."

"Zelda."

"Fuck off." She said it gently. Both of them listened
for a time to the soft random noises of the long-distance line. "Are you all right, Harry?" she said.

"I take a drink now and then. I watch television a lot.
I'm going to be forty-nine the day after tomorrow."

"What does that mean?"

"I'm getting old."

"So who isn't? Come on, Harry, stop making yourself
into a special case."

"I am a special case. How many Harry Caudills do
you know? When I die, who's left?"

"You go through this every birthday—you just don't
remember it from one year to the next."

"Do you and this guy have any kids?" he said.

"Two. I wrote and told you both times."

"Oh yeah," he said.

"That's what I mean. You don't remember things.
You're in a different world, Harry. You're not normal."

"That's what I'm trying to tell you. A special case."

She laughed as easily as if nothing had ever gone wrong between them, no stemmed glasses thrown at the wall in helpless anger, no ugly screaming battles, none of the final spasms of the marriage. He almost called her Zelda again before he remembered that she hated it.

Jo-Lynn was absent from his morning class. When the bell rang Harry opened the anthology he was using as a text and without preamble began to read out loud. His voice fell on the carpeted floor and died without an echo. A boy in the front row yawned; another laid his head on his hands and closed his eyes; two girls by the window began a conversation in loud whispers.

Harry raised his voice. " 'He was ordered to change places with the Jews.' " A white-faced blonde opened her purse, took out a compact, and began to trace a scarlet line on her upper lip.

" 'No prayers or incense rose up in those hours,' " Harry read. Done with her upper lip the girl began with great concentration to paint the lower with slow strokes of her brush.

When he came out in the hall they were waiting for him. Jo-Lynn smiled; the boy nodded to Harry familiarly. "I've forgiven her—we're going to be married." He pulled up the hand he was holding and showed Harry the ring on Jo-Lynn's finger.

"Congratulations," Harry said. He made an effort to speak normally, but his voice sounded in his ears like the wooden clapper on Marvella's weather vane, loud and stupid.

"I love her," the boy said. Emotion seemed to have made his voice go slack.

"Clackety-clack," Harry said. *I hope you'll be happy* were the words that actually came out, but he hardly heard them.

Later he sat on his front steps with a beer in his hand and watched the sun go down on the flat country that stretched toward Columbus. It hung like a red ball for a long time, seemingly without moving, like a miracle, then suddenly, between two sips of Iron City beer, it took the plunge and was gone, leaving Ohio in the dark.

"They hate us," Harry thought. "Oh God how they hate us. They'd murder us all in a minute if they thought they could." He drained the can and threw it overhand across the street; it tumbled queerly in the streetlight's glare and fell into the unnatural woods.

When he finally saw that he wasn't going to be able to sleep he picked up the telephone and called the first woman he'd married. She lived in Los Angeles but the connection was spectrally clear; her voice came to Harry with uncanny precision, undiminished by distance.

"We had some good times," he said.

"We did. I'm sorry it got so complicated." She stopped and Harry said nothing. "Harry?"

"I'm still here."

"I haven't found anybody better . . ."

"I haven't found anybody at all," he told her.

"But I'm glad I left. You're a son of a bitch, Harry; that's what made it complicated."

"There must be some truth to that," he said. "It seems to be a common opinion among women I've known."

"I used to think it was because you were a poet; now I'm pretty certain that you'd be a son of a bitch even if you were a plumber. I don't even think you can help it—it's your nature."

"I forgot about your voice," he said. "You always had a voice that could make me roll over and bark at the moon. I wish you were here now so we could fool around a little."

"Me too," she said. "But it wouldn't change anything. You're a lousy person, Harry, even though you're a charmer. And someday you're going to suffer for it."

"We're all going to suffer," he said. "That's what life is about."

"Don't give me your half-assed pessimism. I mean you *personally* are going to bleed," she said. "And you know what I'll be doing? I'll be laughing."

The sincerity of her anger made him wince; he wanted to hang up the phone, but instead he found himself waiting for her to say something more. There was a long pause. The weather vane clacked once faintly; the sound reminded Harry of Marvella and he wondered how much longer he'd be able to elude her.

"Harry?" his first wife said. "Harry, are you there? Are you all right?"

Only then was he able to break the connection and go to sleep.

Home Is the Blue Moon Cafe

U sed to be I liked the Texas heat, but I don't anymore, so I stepped inside quick. The swamp cooler was making its same stupid whang-whang-whang noise it had been making two years ago, the day I left. Everything else hadn't changed either. The booths with the high backs, the bar, the flypaper, the yellow walls were the same. The way the electric light fell across the stools and lay across the floor in patches and streaks was the dumbest thing I'd ever seen.

Estrellita came out of the ladies' room; I laid down my duffel bag and waited for her to see who it was. She squealed and ran up and threw her arms around me. I looked over her shoulder at Jaime, who was sitting at the bar. Estrellita played at letting the kiss get better; she bit my lip and smoothed over the hurt with her tongue. I added it to the list of things which I had liked before but which now were awkward. Jaime was watching us; he didn't recognize me right away, but he didn't seem to care who was kissing his sister.

She took a half-step away. "I suppose you think you're going to take up with me where you left off, you son of a bitch," she said. "Well you can forget it. I've got a boyfriend and he'll whip your ass if he sees you kiss me like that."

"Hello, Estrellita," I said.

"Not one stinking letter," she said.

"I was pretty busy."

"Shooting people who never did you any harm," she said.

"Elder!" Jaime said. He put down his beer and stood up. "Hey, everybody, it's Elder. When did you get back?"

"Just now," I said.

Frenchy Leroux held out his hand. He was clutching his pool cue and a cigarette together in the other fist. I remembered Frenchy; he wore dark glasses all the time, in or out-of-doors. "You didn't even go home first?" he said, pointing at my bag.

"I've been home," I said. "I just didn't stay."

"I bet it feels good to be back in the US of A," George said. I shook his hand across the bar.

"Is Estrellita crazy or something?" I asked Jaime.

"Oh, man, don't let's get into that. It doesn't matter she's my sister anymore. She's a modern woman now— she does just like she pleases. I'm not responsible."

"Everybody have a beer on the house," George said.

"Did you shoot lots of women?" Estrellita said.

"Only when I couldn't find any babies to blow up," I said. "What's the matter with you?"

"Her new boyfriend is a pacifist," Frenchy said.

"Yeah? Then how come he's going to whip my ass if I kiss you?" I asked Estrellita. She favored me with a disgusted look.

"He's only peaceful when it comes to foreign wars," Jaime said. "Around home he carries a piece of motorcycle chain in his back pocket."

"He's a Devil's Disciple," George said.

His round face floated in the half-dark behind the bar, grinning foolishly. The beer he gave me tasted flat; the shape of the glass it was in made me feel depressed.

"It sure is good to see you again," he said. "We were afraid you'd get hurt in that crazy war."

"This place looks like a rat hole," I said. "Did you ever think about painting the walls something besides puke-yellow? Why don't you sweep the floor once in a while?"

"Same old Elder," George said. He was always happy when he was behind the bar and sober; when he was drunk he suffered from world-gloom.

From the darkest part of the room, behind the pool table, came a tremendous belch.

"Touchstone?" I said.

"Elder my man." Nothing back there stirred—there was just the voice. "I was betting you'd get your ass shot to pieces and get shipped home in a bag."

"I thought you didn't allow niggers in this cafe," I said to George.

Estrellita came back to where I was sitting and punched me on the arm. "We weren't done talking," she said.

"What's a modern woman?" I said. "How do you get to be one?"

"Did you have any whores over there?" she wanted to know.

"Now and then."

"Oh shit," she said. "Why did you have to go in the Army anyhow? You could have gone to the university like Jaime."

Something heavy moved behind the pool table. A chair creaked. "Cause he was a man," Touchstone said. "College is for little boys."

"Hey listen . . ." Jaime said.

"Look at you now," I said, watching Touchstone

come out into the light. "You put on another fifty pounds while I was gone."

He walked carefully around the table; he carried himself like a sumo wrestler, proud of his weight. His belly brushed against a chair and knocked it over.

"Glorious, ain't it?" he said. "There's enough of me to make three or four little shits like Jaime here. Step aside, boy."

"Who you calling boy?" Jaime said. "I could whip your big ass in a minute."

"Everybody have another beer," George said. "On account of Elder getting back safe."

"What are you going to do now?" Estrellita wanted to know. She had slipped into the high-backed booth beside me and was pressing her leg against mine in a way that said love. "What are you going to do now that you're back?"

Home was what I had tried first. When my mama opened the front door and saw me, she started crying.

"It's such a surprise," she said.

My daddy put down the newspaper. "We knew you weren't dead because the Army didn't send us a telegram," he said.

"I wrote you."

"Postcards," he said. "Chinese temples. 'Having a great time, wish you were here.'"

"It was just done in fun," I said.

"It wasn't funny to your mama."

"I'm sorry," I said.

"Was it terrible over there?" my mama said.

"No."

"We saw it on the TV," she said. "You don't have to lie to make us feel better."

"It was only bad now and then," I said.

"Did you ever have to go down in one of those tun-

nels after them?" she said. "I was always afraid you
would have to do that."

"We had specialists. People who got to like the tun-
nels after a while. The rest of us didn't have to do
much but stand around and maybe pull them out.
Crazy niggers, mostly."

"I never raised you to talk like that," my daddy said.

"I'm sorry."

"What's wrong with you?"

"Leave him alone, Hondo," my mama said. "He's just
come back." She sat down on the sofa next to me.
"Don't mind Hondo. He was real worried about you."

"What time is it?" I said a little bit later.

"Something wrong with your eyes too?" Hondo said.
"The clock's hanging on the wall in front of you where
it's been for fifteen years. Quarter to six."

"I have to be going now," I said.

"You're no good," Hondo said.

When I got as far as the door I looked back and saw
my mama crying again; I didn't have any idea in the
world how to get back across that living room to help
her, or what words I could say if I got that far. I threw
my bag over my shoulder and went out. Cutting across
the grass, all I could think of was how stupidly straight
our street was—you could see from one end of it to the
other, for miles.

"So what are you going to do?" Estrellita said.

"I give up," I said. "What?"

"My man," Touchstone said. He leaned over the
back of the booth; the wood cracked and the light over
the table swayed.

"Get off," Frenchy said. He leaned farther; his face
hung between Frenchy and Jaime like a wrecker's ball.
His eyes were closed; his nose was as big as an orange
and the skin stretched over it was pebbled like an

orange rind, but the color of it was a deep serious black.

"Get away," Jaime said. "You smell like a horse."

"I smell like a man, you mean." His eyes opened. The whites were a powerful yellow, crisscrossed by blood vessels; they looked like a rich map of a complicated country. Slowly the head went up and disappeared above the light. He reappeared at the open end of the booth, stuck a chair between his legs, and let himself down.

"You're going to die of fatness," Frenchy said.

"Why're you mean-mouthing me? Didn't I save your good looks last week when Estrellita's boyfriend was going to stomp your face?"

"I could have handled him," Frenchy said.

"You were lying on the parking lot and he was about to put a motorcycle boot across your nose," Jaime said. "You didn't look like you were handling him too good."

"Frank wouldn't really have hurt him," Estrellita said.

"He sneak-punched me." Frenchy squinted at Touchstone. "If you hadn't got in the way I would have killed him. I was *waiting* for him to try and kick me—I know some moves."

"What are you going to do now you're back home?" Jaime said to me.

"Give the boy a chance," George said. "He hasn't even been back a whole day yet. Let him get used to being in God's country."

"It's God's country over there too," Estrellita said.

"If there was a God," Jaime said.

"Since you went to college you don't believe anything anymore," she said.

George leaned forward. "Are you going to tell us how it was over there?"

"You don't want to know."

"Tell it," Touchstone said. He had been in Vietnam himself, in the early days, before things got out of hand. He had already been back two years before I left. He had a Frankenstein scar on his neck, under the right ear, a long bent line, puckered and purple, with little pale dots on both sides where the stitches had been put in to hold him together.

"It's grotesque," Estrellita said when we saw she was staring at it.

"Aaargh," Touchstone said. He rolled his eyes and dangled his head on one side, giving an imitation of a man with his throat cut.

"I just want to know how it really was," George said. "The stuff you don't see on the TV."

"It was Saturday night all the time," I said. "We laid around and rolled joints and drank Lone Star beer and every now and then we fired off a few M-16 rounds into the brush to keep the mamasans and the papasans on their toes. Sometimes we just sat and listened for the B-52's to come over, but that wasn't much good because they fly so high you can't see them or hear them."

"You pigs," Estrellita said. She got up from beside me and went to sit by herself at the end of the bar.

"God loves you, baby," Touchstone said to her. She glared at him. He fingered his scar affectionately and let his tongue hang out; it was orange, thick and floppy like an old mattress, full of ridges and cracks.

"That is the ugliest thing I ever saw," Frenchy said. "Didn't I warn you about that bad mouth?"

"You're big," Frenchy said, "but I'm quick. I'll hit you eight or nine times before you know it's a fight going on."

"That's right," Estrellita said. "Go on and kill each other. That'll prove something, won't it?"

George came over with his rag and wiped our table; he stopped in front of me. "Was that it? Was that all there was to it?"

George is a medium-built man; people who don't know him think he's fat, but he's only soft. He'd been soft as long as I had known him. I had known them all for a long time: Jaime the longest. In second grade I had almost put his eye out with a paperclip.

"Tell me," George said. He was stalled in front of me with his cloth pressed to the table and a filter Kool in his mouth, letting the smoke curl up stupidly into the light of the lamp.

"The gooks don't care if they die," I said. "They carry satchel charges strapped on their backs and they lie down on our barbed wire and blow themselves up to make an opening for their friends. The next morning we'd have to send out details to collect the arms and legs hanging on the wire or lying on top of the bunkers. If we found whole heads we'd boil them down in trash cans for the skulls and sell them to the rear troops for war souvenirs."

"Yes," Touchstone said. He had a weird little laugh, high-pitched and crazy sometimes.

The telephone rang. "It's your mama," George said. He handed the receiver across the bar to Jaime; Jaime gave it to me.

"Hondo's sorry he got on you like that, Elder. He says if you come home he'll be nice."

"Sure," I said. "I'm not leaving town. I'll come to the house sometime."

"He really is sorry."

"He's my daddy—he can say anything to me he wants to," I told her.

"He's telling me right now he wants you to come home."

"Tell him I appreciate that," I said. I gave the phone back to George.

"One for the road?" he said.

"What road is that?" I wasn't going anywhere. "If my daddy wants to see me he could jump in his Thunderbird with the red leather seats and come out to the Blue Moon himself." It goes without saying he won't; he doesn't think it's a respectable place. *Trashy*, he calls it, though he's always polite to my friends when he sees them in the street.

"Your mama sounded pretty sad," George said.

"Why don't you mind your own business and run this sorry place instead of telling me about my mama?"

"Take it easy," Jaime said.

"You can go to hell too."

"You don't like your daddy much," Touchstone said.

"He's my daddy. If I like him or not is my affair, ain't it?"

I went back and shot a couple of games of eight-ball with Frenchy; he left me with about four or five balls on the table every time. He shoots with a closed bridge, which I have been taught to believe isn't as good as the other way, where you make a hollow by holding your thumb stiff and let the stick ride free. But he has a smooth, beautiful stroke and the cue ball moved like it had eyes. I used to love the game of pool—don't know why I never saw before how senseless it was.

I stepped back and bumped into Jaime. "Watch it," I said. "I'm making a shot."

"Watch it yourself," Jaime said.

"To hell with it. I can't shoot anyhow. Something's the matter with my eyes; I can't see across the table to where the balls are. Is that the six-ball over there, Frenchy?"

"The eight."

"I quit," I said. "Here, take your dollar and a half. I can't even tell the damn colors any more."

"Come on and sit with me," Estrellita said. She dragged me back into the same booth. "Kiss me now," she said. She rubbed her leg against mine.

"If Frank saw us he'd kill both of us for sure," she said.

"Yeah?"

"He gets crazy when I even look at another boy."

"Is this a thrill for you?" I said. "Telling me what Frank's going to do when he catches us?"

"He's not going to catch us," she said. "We're not going to do this any more. Don't think you can just come back after two years without writing to me and just jump in where you were."

"OK," I said. "I'll leave you to Frank."

"He's not really like the other Devil's Disciples," she said. "He joined because he says they're really a tribe and tribes are the most functional social organizations."

"A thinker," I said.

"He dropped out of college because they couldn't teach him anything." She picked up my hand and laid it on her leg. "He was going to write a book, but he changed his mind. The really great geniuses, like Jesus and Socrates, never wrote anything down. Writing is just a way to tell lies, Frank says."

"Jesus!" I said.

"Socrates either," she told me. "Never wrote anything. Disciples wrote down what they said."

The door opened. I thought it was Hondo at first, but he was too tall—Hondo's shorter than me. I was squinting against the light coming through the door. George was making little signals with his hands.

"What's wrong with George?" I said to Estrellita.

She stood up. "Over here, Frank."

"Peace," he said to me. He looked like a nice boy; the length of motorcycle chain hanging out of his back pocket was shiny like it had been cleaned with solvent. He had a serious face but didn't look very bright.

"How are you?" I said.

"Elder's an old friend," Estrellita said. "We went together in high school."

"I hear you're into teaching," I said.

"Yeah. Sometimes."

"And Estrellita."

"What?"

"I hear you're into Estrellita too." I smiled up at him.

"Wait a minute now," Jaime said. "You can't talk about my sister."

"She's a modern woman," I said. "Remember?"

"You want to fight?" Frank said.

"He's quick, isn't he?" I said. "Yeah, I want to fight."

"What for?"

"Who cares?" I said. "Does it make a difference?"

He reached for his chain but Touchstone was already pulling it out of his back pocket. He gave it to George to put behind the bar.

"We do it formal here," George said.

"Each of you gets one hit at a time," Touchstone said. "You can duck, but the first man who moves his feet is the loser."

"Call it," Jaime told Frank.

"Heads," Frank said.

Touchstone laid the quarter on his arm. "It's George Washington," he said. "You get to choose. You want to hit first or get hit?"

Frank hit me in the mouth and split my lip. I hit him in the stomach. When he got himself standing straight again he hit me in the mouth one more time. If you know how to roll your head to one side it generally won't knock you down, but it sure does hurt. I was beginning to feel better already. I hit him a round-house on the ear, and water came out of his eyes, but he stayed up.

"You're allowed as long as you want between hits," Touchstone explained to him.

He hit me in the stomach when I wasn't ready, and I lost my breath. I thought my eyes were going to pop out of my head because I was trying so hard to suck in any air at all, but I didn't think I'd gone down until I happened to notice I was on my knees.

"I didn't move my feet," I said after a while.

"He's right," Touchstone said. His face leaned down close to mine and the big yellow eyes looked me over carefully. "You sure you know what you're doing, now?"

"Yeah."

I heard the front door. I closed my eyes for a second to concentrate on breathing. "In trouble again," my daddy's voice said.

"Mr. Skinner," Frenchy said.

"Call me Hondo," my daddy said politely. "What's all this here about?"

"They're fighting over me," Estrellita said. She was leaning forward on her barstool, trying not to miss anything.

"Wrong," I said. "What this is, is a philosophy lesson."

I got up on one knee first, then the other, careful not to move my feet. As soon as I felt steady I hit Frank on the ear again. He cried a little more, then he hit me in the same place in the stomach and this time my feet went their own way and I cracked the back of my head on the booth.

When I took an interest in things again, Frank and

Estrellita were gone. Hondo was standing over me; his face had no expression.

"Can you hear me?" he said.

I waggled my hand, meaning yes.

He held his hat in front of him; he'd had it ever since I could remember him—a gray Stetson with a high crown. He wasn't really my daddy; he'd married my mama three months after I was born, when my real daddy had left her to go with a waitress from Amarillo. On the other hand he was the only daddy I had, and he and my mama hadn't had any kids, so Hondo had to be satisfied with me too.

I felt pretty damn good, at least for the time being, lying there on the floor of the Blue Moon Cafe. Hondo pulled a white handkerchief out of his breast pocket and gave it to me to wipe the blood out of my mouth.

"Your mama thinks I drove over here to ask you to come home," he said. He squatted down beside me, still holding his hat. His voice was low and serious. "You can if you want to, but I don't give a damn what you do. Stay away and you'll break your mama's heart, but I know if you come home you'll break it anyhow."

I waggled my hand again.

"So what's it going to be?" he said.

"Yes," I said.

"You going to come home?"

"I don't know," I said. "Give me a minute." I smiled at him and started my lip bleeding again.

"You ain't much good," he said.

"I'm all you got," I told him.

"Ain't it the truth," Touchstone said.

The Amelia Barons

In the picture I keep in my head my father wears his old blue windbreaker unzipped to the waist. On the back, between his shoulders, is printed a knight's helmet with a drooping plume; under the helmet, in Gothic capitals, is the name of the team my dad coached, the Amelia Barons. He is bald on top already; he's shorter than most of the high school boys who stand around him waiting to get into the game. He paces the sidelines and hunches forward to guide a falling football which I remember is going to be tipped high in the air and intercepted.

Families are where you learn how to live, and the lesson has to last a good long time. It takes energy to make a family work, and determination and open-eyed intelligence. My father made *his* work, and I can see now that it wasn't always easy.

Kathleen and I live in Toledo, where I am making it pretty well in the retail lumber and home hardware business. We have a new house in Ottawa Hills with redwood decks and a triple clump of white-barked birch trees growing out of the front lawn. The landscapers threw in a couple of big chunks of split granite that could with a little of the engraver's art be made into a pair of tombstones. We have a color TV in the bedroom, two cars, health insurance and a retirement plan. We're considering a child; we're considering a divorce.

Two years ago my father retired from teaching and moved my mother and himself to Arizona. My wife, who has no living parents, talks to my mother on the long-distance telephone several times a week; she carries the phone to the bedroom so I can't listen. I don't hear very often from my father; when he calls I'm always surprised and a little scared that it's going to be bad news. He generally reaches me at the office.

I leaned back in my chair and watched the boys in the yard unload a trailer of white-wood two-by-fours and two-by-sixes from Georgia Pacific. They don't even bother to tell you what kind of lumber you're getting any more; it could have been Douglas fir, or pine, or hemlock—it's all *white-wood* now, and twice the price it was only a year ago.

"How's Arizona?"

"Beautiful," my father said. "It's a whole new life out here." Something in the long-distance electronics gave his voice an echo, as if he was speaking to me from the bottom of a cave. There was something else in his tone. A warning.

"What's wrong?" I said.

"Nothing. Does something have to be wrong before I can call you? I just wanted to talk to you."

"Listen," I said, "things are pretty slack around here just now, and I could use a couple days vacation. Why don't I fly out this weekend?"

"I'll pick you up at the airport." He sounded relieved. "Wait until you see the mountains."

I looked it up the other day. In twenty-two years of coaching the Barons my dad came close to a winning season three times. The Barons were 4 and 5 in 1949, the year I was born; in 1955, when my dad came back from the Korean War, they were 5 and 5; and 4 and 5 again in 1969. In the spring of '71 the school board took the team away from him and gave it to a football player from Utah who had come to Amelia, God knows why, to teach physical education. The board let my father go on teaching chemistry and physics and general science until he had earned his pension, but he never coached again.

In his first year the man from Utah made the boys kneel and pray on the gritty concrete of the locker-room floor before each game; the Barons won seven out of ten. My father watched from the bleachers and cheered every time they scored. My mother sent me a photograph of one of the bonfire pep-rallies and in the background I can make out my dad in his blue windbreaker; it would have been his idea of loyalty and pride.

I thought about him while I sailed in a high arc above the country, knee to knee with salesmen and engineers and other men like myself preoccupied with the world. I realized that I had learned early from watching my father that people who want too much out of life end up with nothing, and I had trimmed my sails accordingly. I could have been a painter or an architect; at one time I thought I could be a sculptor, and in my junior year at Ohio State I took private lessons on the violin. But in the end I played it safe; I wanted to be sure nobody would ever be able to replace me with an ex-linebacker from Utah and break my heart.

My father wanted his team to be a winner, he wanted my mother and me to be happy, he wanted the world to be a good place; he wanted those things too much, and too obviously, so that most people, even his friends, couldn't feel very much at ease around him. But he wasn't a fool, and he was never ridiculous.

When Martin Luther King was shot my dad called to tell me he had driven to Pittsburgh to march with the NAACP in their time of mourning. It was two days after the assassination. On TV during breakfast I had seen buildings in flames near the Golden Triangle, and crowds running from tear gas.

"You could have been killed," I said to him. "What good did you do?"

We held on through a long silence. "At least you did something," I said. "I sat home and felt sorry he was dead."

"How's Kathleen?" my father said.

"She's fine."

"What's wrong?" he said. "You don't sound like yourself."

"Just worries. I worry about losing my job, going broke, not being able to make the payments on the house. Three mornings out of five I wake up in a sweat, with my heart going a mile a minute."

"Are you in some kind of trouble at work?"

"No. It's just a sort of general panic. Don't you ever worry about things like that?"

"I guess I used to when I was your age," he said. But I knew that he was lying to make me feel better. He worried about the world. If my father ever woke up in a sweat it was because of a famine in Africa or police brutality in Alabama. He had a lot of love, but he spread it too thin, on blacks in the South, or Mexicans in California, or on the Amelia Barons.

I looked out at the engines hung under the wing, gulping the thin air and shooting us forward. My dad would probably ask about Kathleen; he'd know from her phone calls that we weren't getting along. I wasn't sure what I could tell him. She was a southern Ohio girl, from Utopia, a river town said to have been the place where Eliza crossed the ice to freedom. I had married her because I thought I loved her, and because among the determined coeds at Ohio State she had seemed beautiful, intelligent, gentle. Now the beauty and the intelligence remained, but the gentleness had flown. She was touchy, irritable, apt to fly into a rage over nothing at all. I spent more time at the office than I needed to; when the weather was good I haunted the golf courses in Maumee and Perrysburg. On Saturdays and Sundays I was gone by seven-thirty in the morning; when I came home the dishes were piled high in the sink, the carpets full of lint, the furniture dusty, my wife angry at nothing. The next morning I'd wake up cold and shaky, adding up my bank balance, calculating my changes.

The stewardess came and I had a drink and another and looked down through the holes in the clouds, trying to make sense of what I saw. I didn't have any idea where we were—it could have been Minnesota, Kansas, Oklahoma. I had looked at the airline map, but I couldn't tell which of the long red curving lines we were riding. In the very hazy distance something gleamed—it could have been a lake; immediately under the plane the ground was a dark dusty green, featureless and primitive.

Sometimes Kathleen looked at me with her face closed tight; she made believe that nothing could touch her; not my misery, not my anger, not the memory of the child we might as well never have.

"Never is a long time," my father used to say.

I remember him at the breakfast table in Amelia, in his tweed jacket and wide blue tie—I must have been nine or ten. He spooned sugar over his cornflakes and looked at me seriously.

"When I grow up I'm never going to be unhappy," I said.

"Never is a long time."

"Don't you think I can do it?"

He held the spoon poised over his bowl. In the background my mother sang under her breath; she broke eggs into a skillet. It was spring, the window was open, and the smell of the trees leafing out made my head soar with certainty.

"Maybe *almost* never," my father said.

As soon as he said it I knew I didn't believe it, and I remember feeling uneasy because I sensed that he did, that my father thought if you tried hard enough, wanted it enough, you need almost never be unhappy. He was about thirty-six years old then, and he still had plenty of time to get out of Amelia and out of high school teaching, but his queer mixture of faith and determination defeated him. He wanted too much.

Something else defeated me, I thought. Not wanting enough, maybe. Not loving enough.

The plane swooped down toward Tucson; the clouds had been gone from under us for a while, and we landed in blazing light that made my head ring. Reflections popped around me like flashbulbs. The plane ride had made me dizzy and I came down the ramp and waded out to my father through waves of light.

His place was in Sierra Vista, sixty miles east of Tucson. We drove slowly into the desert; each of us waited for the other to start talking. The flight had seemed to take no time at all and I was surprised to see, so near Toledo, the giant saguaros, taller than men, standing stiff in the red sand with their arms raised to the sky.

"So how's Mom?" I said.

"She's fine." After a while he went on. "She thought I should come by myself to pick you up, so we'd have a chance to talk."

"Is one of you sick?"

"Nothing like that."

I watched the desert unroll outside my window. It looked the same as it does in the movies, except that seeing it like that through tinted glass, with the air-conditioning on, made it seem more remote and strange than it had on the screen. My dad drove like he always had, slowly, with both hands on the wheel, leaning forward to look at the road.

"I don't know why I didn't come out here before," I said.

"You were too busy getting on."

"The mountains are pretty."

"They're incredible," he said. "Do you like what you're doing in Toledo?"

"The business? Sure. No. I don't know—I wouldn't want to do it for the rest of my life."

"Be careful you don't, then," he said.

There were no trees on my father's three acres, though we could see some cottonwoods following the line of a small creek in the distance. A single well served sixteen parcels of land out of a hundred-thousand-gallon sheet-iron tank half-sunk in the caliche soil, as hard as good Toledo concrete. The bunch-grass only half-hid the red dirt. The Chiricahua Mountains and the Dragoon Range were stark and beautiful. I could see why my father liked the place. His house was a two-piece prefabricated cottage; at dinner he told me how it had been hauled all the way from Phoenix on two trailer-trucks, lifted down by the developer's crane and bolted together by sweating Indian laborers.

"Quickest thing you ever saw," he said. "One morning there was nothing there but a concrete pad; by afternoon we had our house."

"I can't get used to not having a cellar," my mother said.

"The only way to dig one would have been with

dynamite," my father said. "Anyway, what do you need a cellar for out here?"

"What if there's a tornado?" she said. "In Ohio we always used to keep a flashlight and some fresh water and canned food downstairs in case of a storm."

"There aren't any tornadoes in Arizona," my father said.

"The water's hard as nails too," she said. "It makes little flakes of stone in the kettle when it boils." Her face didn't lose its cheerful expression, but she began to cry. "I just can't get used to it," she said.

"I'm going for a walk," my father said. When he slammed the door their little house shook as if a high wind had come up.

"He loves it here," my mother said. "But to me it's like a foreign country. I don't know what to do. Would you like some coffee?" When she picked up the kettle to set it on the burner I heard the little pieces of stone rattling in the water.

"I think your father and I might separate," she said.

"You mean just for a while," I said.

"Maybe." She watched the little blue flames under the kettle. "I can't even cook right any more," she said. "We're up at five thousand feet and the water never gets hot enough. I don't know how to boil an egg properly here."

"You and Dad can't get a divorce," I said.

"Of course we can." She dried her eyes and poured the coffee.

"You can't," I said.

"I remember when you were in college," she said. "If you came home and we'd changed anything in the house you'd get furious. Tell me the truth—you were angry when your dad and I sold the house in Amelia and moved out here, weren't you?"

"Of course not," I said.

"Parents have their own lives to lead," she said.

"You're taking all this pretty well," I told her resentfully.

"It's a lot more than just where we live," my father told me as he drove me back to Tucson and the airport. "I'd sell the land and the house and go back to Ohio tomorrow if I thought there was anything to be gained by it."

"Aren't you afraid of being alone?" I said.

"Yes." He stared straight ahead at the road. "I don't want you to feel bad about it. It happens all the time and it isn't the end of the world. People get to where they have nothing left to say to each other sometimes."

I rolled down my window and took a deep breath; even at night the air was superheated. It tasted too thin to support life. "Kathleen and I aren't doing so well either. You probably know all about it already."

"I had a general idea," my father said.

"We get into actual fistfights sometimes, like two little kids. She bites—I could show you the marks. I get so mad I can't see straight, and she's even worse. You and Mom never did that."

"Different generations," he said. "Only lower-class people hit each other in those days. Or movie stars, like Bogart and Bacall."

We had come to the Interstate and my father slowed the car to take the on-ramp. The headlights swept along the guardrail; beyond the galvanized metal was darkness except for a thin band of pure turquoise on the horizon.

"You and Mom," I said. "It's going to take some getting used to."

"I didn't want to tell you over the telephone," he said.

We shook hands at the terminal gate. "Have a good flight," he said. "Go on home and do the best you can. Don't worry about us."

Half-way up the aluminum steps to the plane I turned and ran back down past the other passengers. My father was still there, under the lights. I threw my arms around him as if I was making an open-field tackle.

"Jesus, Dad," I said. "I'm sorry. I'm really sorry." I held him tight. We were in the middle of the door and people in a hurry pushed to get around us.

"I'm sorry too," he said.

I took a taxi home from the airport. I turned on the living room lights; newspapers were scattered on the floor; there was an empty cup on the coffee table, a half-full glass of water on the arm of a chair. I heard Kathleen talking on the phone in the bedroom.

"I'm home," I said.

"I'll be out in a minute."

I picked up yesterday's sports page. The Pirates were down in the second division and losing ground. The writers blamed it on Manny Sanguillen, who is probably the best catcher in the majors. The New York Giants had made an off-season trade for another quarterback. I've followed them since their glory days in the late fifties, when my dad and I used to watch them on Sunday afternoon TV. They could resurrect Y. A. Tittle and it wouldn't help them now, but I still watch them. Out of loyalty, I guess.

Kathleen came out and let herself be kissed. "How's Mother?" I said.

"How would you expect her to be? He's leaving her after thirty years."

"I thought she was leaving him, as much as anything."

"That's *his* story." She sat on the edge of the couch. Her face was closed against me. "Naturally he's not going to tell you it's his fault."

"Let's not get into a fight about it," I said.

"Men are all bastards," she said.

On slow Mondays I have a lot of time to think. The yard is quiet, with maybe a couple of one-horse remodeling contractors hunting through the stacks for cheap two-by-fours or marked-down fencing cedar. In the office the secretaries yawn and do their nails. The salesmen pour themselves another cup of coffee they don't want, and lean against the displays of paint and plumbing supplies, hand-tools, and hardware. Over in electrical Harry Calder, who sometimes plays golf with me, is half asleep. He's looking out at the street past a pair of Toro mowers in the window, which we'll probably never sell, and his face is full of gloom.

Kathleen and I are probably not going to stick it out. The house in Ottawa Hills is enormous for two people, but we bump into each other as inevitably as if we were still in the efficiency apartment we lived in during my senior year at Ohio State. Each bump leaves a bruise, painful and slow to heal.

My dad is what I guess I would call a good man, but he never really succeeded in life, and until this Monday morning I realized that I had always held it against him. Now I saw that for all my trimming my sails to conform to what I thought was the way of the world, I wasn't going to do any better than he had. Maybe a good deal worse. He kept his family together as long as there was any reason to. He taught me to love, even though he spread it out too thin. He was a good coach to the Barons; if nothing else, he taught them how to

lose the big game and come out for practice the next
Monday afternoon with a good heart.

He did this without becoming outrageous. I read in
the sports section last year about a coach in Florida
who made his players stomp chickens on the locker-
room floor to wake up their blood-lust. While we
waited to tee off one Sunday morning Harry Calder
told me that his high school coach once ate the head
off a live frog at half-time in front of his kids; they
were losing the homecoming game by two touchdowns
and he wanted to give them the power of unreason by
his example, I suspect. The Barons' new coach makes
them pray. My father talked to the Barons quietly and
seriously, wanting to make them win out of the rational
desire to be better. He told them they could win in the
same tone in which he told me that it was possible, if I
tried hard, to almost never be unhappy in life.

He loved football with an intensity that those of us
who watch it on television or play two-hand touch in the
park can't begin to understand. He didn't see it as a
metaphor for life; his love was uncomplicated by outside considerations; I think he saw it simply as a com-
petitive art, like chess. Like a good artist, he was conser-
vative; he played the single-wing for years after every
other school in our part of the state had abandoned it
for the seductive, decadent fluidity of T-formation football. His teams lost, but they lost without, like so many
poor teams, becoming fancy, foolish and wild, and losing pride in themselves.

Today or tomorrow or next month he'll phone and
tell me they're going through with the divorce. And in
a year or two or five, another call will tell me he's dead.
In the meantime I'm going to try to make it up with
Kathleen and have that child. We'll get the divorce too,

but on weekends I'll take my son to the aquarium or to the zoo, or we'll sit home and watch the Giants and their new quarterback lose to Philadelphia or Dallas. I'll explain to him about the Amelia Barons, and how everybody loses, even Utah ex-linebackers who have God, and how the thing is to do it with dignity and keep your pride, which is not a sin, but the only true virtue we have, the root of all other virtues. I'll tell him about his father's father.

A Hunk of Burning Love

Gene is already there when I come through the door of the New Deal Cafe and Bar. There's a sausage speared on the end of his fork and he's waving it in Rita's face. Gene's a fat man but a long way from jolly; he can in fact be mean as a snake if you give him half a chance. His hat is on the stool beside him, upside down with his work gloves folded in it. This morning we'll be digging postholes for a new fence in old man Hazzard's pasture.

"This sausage looks more like a dog turd," he says.

I like Rita. We have been to bed together now and then, after a hard Saturday night, in her little trailer out back of the cafe.

"Ease up, Gene," I tell him.

He turns around on the stool and gives me his Monday-morning stare, cold and nasty, as if I was some Dallas-Fort Worth traveling salesman cutting in on his time, instead of the man he has been working alongside of, off and on, for the past three years since I came down from Chicago.

"Can I have the number three?" I ask Rita. "And lots of coffee?"

Gene is still giving me the stare. "I know what you've been doing," he says.

"What's that?"

"Never mind," he says. "I know, that's all."

"Eat your breakfast," I tell him. "It's going to be a hard day. Mellow out, buddy."

He looks after Rita, who is jiggling her way into the kitchen with my order. "Yeah?" he says.

His eyes show white all around like a spooky horse. I'm watching him carefully, ready to slide off my stool and give him room, but he blinks and heaves a big sigh. "One of these times they are by pure accident going to get somebody back there that knows how to cook and then I am going to have to start eating my breakfast in some other cafe because my stomach couldn't stand the surprise. Dog turds," he says, shoving the sausage in his mouth and chewing loud enough to make the salesmen at the table behind us turn around and look.

Gene looks back at them and smiles his best affable smile; they have the good sense to smile back.

Rita puts my breakfast down in front of me and swipes at the counter with a wet cloth. "Don't mind him," she says.

As soon as we get settled in the truck Gene slips the same old eight-track in the stereo; we ride the fifteen miles out to Hazzard's property listening to "Hound Dog" and "Blue Suede Shoes" and the rest of this tormented music that Gene likes so well.

He lights up a joint big as a dollar cigar and passes it across to me. In no time we are driving along in a cloud so thick it's a wonder he can find the road through the windshield.

"It was all them drugs give him by Jewish doctors," Gene says. "That killed him, I mean."

"How do you know they were Jewish?"

"I read about it," he says. "You telling me they weren't?"

"I don't know."

"You don't know much," he says.

His truck is an old four-wheel-drive Ford with balloon tires and a worn-out suspension; every little bump sends us swooping across the highway almost into the ditch on the far side.

"You think I'm some kind of bigot, don't you?" he says.

"No."

"Yeah you do."

"Watch the road," I tell him. "It's all right."

"No it ain't all right." He takes a deep drag, adds to the cloud. The truck bounces; Elvis sings. The heater is on and I feel dopey and too warm.

"The King," Gene says finally. "Being from Chicago you wouldn't know what that means."

"Why not? I watched Elvis the first time he was ever on TV, on the Ed Sullivan Show. I know the songs."

"Nope," Gene says. His voice is final. It reminds me of the bumper sticker on his tailgate. GOD SAID IT. I BELIEVE IT. THAT SETTLES IT. In blue and yellow. Not that I've ever heard of him going to church; he's religious in a patriotic, formal kind of way. It goes with the Confederate flag on the other side of the tailgate. I kidded him about fighting losing battles once, until he got mad, but it seems to me that's what the South is all about—how to get beaten and somehow come out on top morally.

"You been living down here with real folks three years now," Gene says. "You wear Dingo boots and a big buckle on your belt, and I taught you to drink Lone Star, but that don't mean you *know.*"

Somebody coming the other way in a station wagon honks his horn and flashes the lights to tell us to get back on our own side of the road. Gene gives them the finger without letting himself get worked up about it.

The King sings about the child born in the ghet-to. Gene turns him down.

"Hey, Lawrence," he says.

"Larry," I tell him for the hundredth time.

"Law-rence," he says. "You ever think what it's all about? Life, I mean. You ever stop to think how we're all going to die?"

"Monday's always bad," I tell him. "We'll be there in a minute and we'll work up a good sweat. You'll feel better."

"No," he says. "I don't think I will."

The tape is hung up between tracks and I give it a kick to get it started again, and turn up the volume; I'd rather listen to Elvis than to Gene getting himself spooked by life.

"I ought to be running fence around my own place instead of old man Hazzard's," he says. "Have some kids. You ever have kids, Lawrence?"

"Two."

"Where they at?"

"Chicago."

"You just left them there?" He shakes his head as if he can't believe a man could do such a thing.

By lunchtime we are down to just pants and boots. It's January and not much above freezing but we have worked up a fine sweat putting up half a dozen lengths of new split-rail. Hazzard's pasture is mostly what they call *caliche*, hard as good Chicago cement. Here and there a little bit of bunch-grass rises out of it, barely alive. It's a pasture the same way the New Deal Cafe is a restaurant.

Gene stretches out on the ground and uncaps a Lone Star. He hasn't said anything for the past couple of hours, but I can tell it's still Blue Monday.

"You and Rita," he says.

"What about me and Rita?"

He rubs his thumb and forefinger together and grins. "I know what you've been doing."

"It's no secret."

"I guess not," he says. We both stare at the sky, which is, like most always, enormous and blue. Now and then down here there is some sort of weather, usually violent. The rest of the time the sky is like a TV screen when the station is off the air, a blank waiting to be filled in.

"Not that I give a damn," Gene says.

"About Rita and me?"

"That's right," he says. He sits up and drinks the rest of the bottle in one gulp and throws the empty carefully into the back of the pickup, with the fenceposts, the rusty tools, the other empties.

With his shirt off Gene looks pretty bad, though I can see how strong he still is. But everything is beginning to slump and settle and dry out and crack. His chest looks like the fields out there after a hard rain and a couple of days of sun.

"Gene?"

"You son of a bitch," he says.

About four o'clock I am taking a turn with the digging bar, a piece of wrought iron six feet long and as big around as an axe handle, which we use to break up the caliche before we can dig it out. Gene is leaning on the two-handled scoop waiting for me to get done.

"Indians," he says.

"What about Indians?"

"There used to be Indians all around here," he says.

I take another shot at the caliche. The bar feels like it weighs a hundred pounds. "What happened to them?"

Gene looks at me like I've asked a dumb question.

"They died out," he says. "Or they went someplace else. See any Indians in Chicago?"

"I guess so."

"That's what I should do," he says. "Go someplace else."

"And do what?" I ask him. If I could only talk to Gene I think something important might happen. But it's a dream: I can't talk to him.

"I can't tell until I got there, Lawrence," he says.

We dig for a while. He takes a turn; I take a turn. Over our heads the sky is like a page from a book that hasn't been written.

"Sometimes you can find old bones out here. I found a tooth once," Gene says. He fumbles in his pocket and brings out a little piece of yellow ivory; it looks like a tooth from a six-year-old. "Indian," he says, holding it out to me cupped in his hand.

It feels so light it has no consequence at all. "Probably a thousand years old," he says. "I was going to have it made into a ring but I never did."

I hand it back to him, but he shakes his head. "Keep it," he says. "Give it to Rita, she likes stuff like that."

"You're sore about me and Rita, aren't you?"

"No," he says.

He's standing in front of me with the bar raised, ready to take another lick at the hole. With his arms up like this, his chest looks like a young man's: not so devastated. We're out here about fifteen miles from nowhere, just Gene and me alone. The muscles are like blow-up balloons. Put a pipe in his mouth and he'd look like Popeye. He could kill me without thinking about it, and your average Texas jury would let him off with a year or two.

"I lost her fair and square," he says. "Before you ever come down here from Chicago. She don't believe in love." His face is both sad and puzzled; the whites of his eyes are showing. There might be a tear in his eye, or it might be only the wind, which is blowing cold and mean, coming from that part of the world Gene doesn't believe in. "Well, Law-rence," he says. "It's about time to quit for the day. Let's go home."

In the truck we listen to Elvis some more but Gene doesn't talk. He drives it slow and easy, listening to the King, nodding his head now and then as if he's just said something to himself that he agrees with. The stereo is going bad and sometimes Elvis comes out from the left speaker, or the right, or quits altogether until I kick the dashboard and get him singing again. I get my feet as close to the heater as I can; now that I'm just sitting I'm cold and a little puzzled and sad myself. I wish we had this day over again, so we could do it different.

"You're a dumb-ass, Law-rence," Gene says.

It's like a judgment; he might be right. I'm not feeling any better about the day. We're sitting in the New Deal Cafe and Bar; it's two in the morning and all but a couple of really serious drinkers have gone home for the night.

"A real dumb-ass," he says.

One of the drunks puts a half-dollar in the jukebox and picks out a tune.

"Seems like that's all anybody plays any more since he died," Rita says.

Gene looks up at her. "We could still get ourselves married," he says.

"Time for you to go on home when you start talking like that." She puts a hand over his. "Go get yourself some sleep," she says. We have been taking turns explaining this day to her, and it's clear she doesn't like the sound of it any more than we do.

"Love," Gene says. He waves his free hand at the jukebox; the drunk is leaning on it, staring at the record going round and round, caught up in some kind of personal tragedy.

"Don't you care about love?" Gene says.

"No," Rita says.

"I can't believe that," he says.

"Go home, Gene," she tells him.

The King is singing "Jailhouse Rock" and Gene does a clumsy little dance step on his way out of the New Deal; he stops at the door and waves good-bye to us, then he stops grinning and gives me a narrow look.

"Chicago," he says. He rubs his thumb and forefinger together and nods at Rita without taking his eyes off me. It's his Monday-morning stare.

Rita's trailer is about fifteen feet long, and set up like one room, with a bed smack up against the back wall and a little kitchen up front. There's a tiny toilet, but if she wants to take a shower she has to go into the cafe, where there's a tin stall behind the kitchen that the help can use. It isn't much of a place to live, but I've been in there with her one or two times when it was pouring rain and lightning and thundering, and it's the coziest thing you can imagine, lying in the bed listening to the water and the wind beating on the sheet-metal six inches away from your head while you're warm and safe under the covers.

"It was just a lousy day," I tell her.

"Let me see the tooth," she says. "Is it really a thousand years old?"

I have to reach out and fumble around on the floor until I find my Levis, and there it is in the back pocket. She holds it up to the light.

"That's so goddamned sad," she says.

I put my arm around her; there's plenty of flesh there, too much, some people might say, but tonight I wish there was more, so much I couldn't get my arms around it all. She's a giving woman, but tonight I maybe want more than she can give.

"I like it when you hold me like that," she says.

"Yeah?" My nose is buried in her hair, which smells like cigarette smoke.

"Don't you go thinking about love," she says.

"That's Gene," I tell her. "Not me."

"Let it sell the songs," she says. "I don't want any of it in my personal life."

"You don't have to worry about me."

"That's what I hope," she says.

After a while she gets up and turns off the overhead light, leaving the little lamp on over the kitchen sink, and we make love, very slow and sweet, driving it easy, and go to sleep tangled up with each other. One of her legs is over mine, my arm is under her head, and with my free hand I'm holding her breast, which is a comfort.

What wakes me up is at first not clear. The trailer is rocking a little but I figure it's in my head, a hangover from the dream I was having in which every one of old man Hazzard's fenceposts was rising slowly out of the ground. In the dream I didn't want to know what was pushing them up. Rita is already sitting, looking around wild-eyed, still more than half in a dream herself.

"It's Gene," she says.

"We were just dreaming," I tell her. "Come on down here and go back to sleep."

I hear footsteps outside and a fist begins to beat slowly on the trailer door; the glasses in the kitchen rattle like dry bones, and something in the sink falls over.

"Rita," Gene's voice says, very drunk and very loud. "Rita, honey, it's me."

He begins to pound on the door again, pulls on the handle, rocks our little trailer. It's a big one-man storm going on out there.

"I love you," he shouts. "I know that son of a bitch Lawrence is in there with you, but it don't matter. We'll have kids; I'll build you a regular house. I'll be tender with you. Love me, goddamn it."

He runs around to the other side of the trailer and bangs on the metal wall; it sounds like thunder. Rita puts her hands over her ears. "Oh God," she says. "I can't stand it."

There's a little window just over the bed. I pull the curtain back and look out, but it's too dark—the only thing I can make out is my own face staring back at me with a peculiar lost expression.

"He's going to keep it up, I just know it," Rita says.

The footsteps are coming back around; they stop just under the window. Gene knows where the bed is. He says something but his voice is funny and I can't understand the words.

"What's he doing?" Rita says. She takes her hands away from her ears so she can hear better.

"I think he's singing."

It gets louder and I can start to make it out. I can see him out there, standing on his toes to get his mouth up to the window, one hand pressed on each side of it to keep his balance, hugging our trailer.

"I'm just a hunk, a hunk-a burning love," he sings.

I pull Rita down in the bed beside me and lay the covers over our heads. I put my arms around her. It's the coziest thing you can imagine.

La Vida

Lunchtime. Loveman comes down off his roof. He looks back up, sees the peak of the house he built, and past that the Oregon sky: woolly clouds that remind him of the state university sheep that graze endlessly in the field down the road. Dumb beasts with stenciled numbers on their backs. Loveman hates sheep, for that matter hates this country Rachel insisted on discovering. He wishes he was back in New York.

He takes two steps and trips on a rock no bigger than a gooseturd. Hammer and hatchet hung from his belt punch him in the kidneys and take his breath away. He's not surprised; the world looked OK up there for a minute, but he knows life is a shit sandwich and he'll eat his share before he's done.

He pulls his aching bones together, gets up to go in the house, and trips again over the threshold. He falls three out-of-control steps into his wife's arms and knocks both of them down on the blue carpet. They lie hurt and tangled and stare at each other with wild eyes.

"I hate you," Rachel whispers. "I hate you. Fuck me now."

Later, over the soup, she looks at Loveman with the intensity of Stanley staring at the blank map of Africa.

"You're going to be the greatest thing I ever did," she says. "I'm going to make you famous."

"Why me?"

"Why not you? Could be anybody, Loveman. Just happens I'm living with you. You're handy."

"I hate this," Loveman says.

"Tell me again about Aunt Esther," Rachel says. She makes notes on a piece of paper folded eight times back into itself. He tells her how Aunt Esther once pulled down his pants and stared for a long time at his little prick, then burst into hot tears and ran out of the room. It happened in Loveman's third year. Rachel takes it all down in tiny ballpoint scratches. Loveman can already see his little prick in the *New York Review of Books*. Rachel's a genius; she could do it. Didn't she once hang a painting of nude Loveman, balls and all, in one of New York's best galleries?

He gets up to walk in the living room; his toe catches the edge of the rug and he pitches forward like a sack of potatoes. Something wrong here, he thinks, staring down his nose at the blue fibers growing down into the floor.

"What's the matter with you?" Rachel says.

The doctor is Rachel's friend, a twenty-eight-year-old Puerto Rican girl who clawed her way into Columbia and then Harvard Medical School. Out here in Oregon, people take her seriously, she says. That's why she came.

She sits Loveman on the edge of the examining table with his bare hairy legs hanging down into space, his feet dangling six inches off the cold floor. She taps, gropes, measures, palpates, hums to herself while she studies his carcass.

"How often do you have intercourse?" she says.

"What's that got to do with anything?" Loveman wants to know.

She looks at him with impartial doctor's eyes. "Sometimes this sort of thing is psychosomatic," she says. "Are you unhappy about your life?"

"Isn't everybody?" Loveman says. "Why do I fall over things all the time?"

"Dropfoot."

"What?"

"Your feet don't swing up when you walk."

Loveman looks puzzled.

"Your toes hang down all the time, that's why you trip over everything. Look at me." She walks back and forth in front of him to demonstrate, first like a regular human being, then like a Loveman, toes flopping like loose socks.

"So why?" Loveman says. A cold wind whistles up under the gown and freezes his organs, the same ones, though bigger now, that will be mentioned in the reviews of Rachel's masterpiece.

"The only thing that would do it is if somebody cut certain tendons in your ankle with a scalpel," she tells him. "Either that or a degenerative nervous disease which I don't think you have."

"So if it isn't this and it isn't that, what's left?"

"Nothing," she says.

She has little black eyes, a beak for a nose, kinky hair—it all adds up to beauty and Loveman would like a piece of it, but how can he? She and Rachel are best friends, a sacred bond; they tell each other everything.

"I'll do some reading in the literature," she says. She touches his leg. "Don't worry, I don't think it's anything serious. I'll call you at home next week."

While Loveman is pulling on his pants he hears whispering in the hall; she is talking to Rachel, who waited outside from motives of decency.

On the way home in Rachel's rattling Porsche, Loveman asks her what they talked about. "Schmuck," she says. She shifts into fourth gear in a school zone, scattering first-graders. "You wanted to make her. I was asking her if you tried anything in there. I'll scratch your eyes out."

"I think there's a cop behind us," Loveman says.

A tall polite young man with yellow teeth and a Wyatt Earp mustache. He studies her driver's license, looks Loveman over without pleasure.

"My husband's dying," Rachel says. "We just came from the doctor and found out he has a rare nervous disease. I didn't realize I was going so fast. I didn't know what I was doing."

She works up a tear and promises to be careful in the future. As soon as the cop is gone she takes off with a screech of tires, the Porsche fishtailing furiously in the dead leaves.

"Hicks," she says to Loveman. "Creeps. Why did we ever leave New York?"

"You said a human being couldn't live there," Loveman says. "Am I really dying?"

"We'll know in a week," she tells him. "When Maria calls. In the meantime stay off the damn roof. I'll make you some coffee when we get home and you can tell me more about Aunt Esther. That little scene was good but I want to know what else she did to you."

"Nothing," Loveman says. "She was just a nice old lady who was a little confused about things, that's all."

"Tell Mama," Rachel says. She sweeps around a curve with one hand on the wheel and the other on Loveman's knee. "I need it for the book." She pinches him and Loveman yelps and bangs his knee on the dashboard. "Besides, it'll make you feel better," she says. "It's good to get these things out in the open."

Against her advice he climbs back on the roof, drags his floppy toes up the wooden ladder, squats on the shingles, and hammers and fits, fits and hammers, across the roof and back again like a measuring worm, patient, gaining four inches at a clip, while through the diminishing gap between shingles and ridge-beam comes the tap-tap of Rachel's Smith-Corona.

She never looks up. Her fingers cruise the keyboard, finding words that will alter Loveman in subtle and irreparable ways. He's sitting at such an angle on the roof that his toes are nearly touching his shins. Pain makes him shift his weight a little. He'd like to descend like an angel between the rafters and kiss the pink spot where his wife's hair swirls at the back of her head like the eye of a storm in the weather-satellite photographs. "Hey," he says. "Hey, I'm talking to you." No answer. The fingers down there are probing for his vital spot, looking for the nerve. Loveman sighs, picks up a shingle, fits it along the chalk line, nails it down. No angels up here, just Loveman with his hatchet, his hammer, his apron full of galvanized nails, his desire not to be made into a book. He leans down until his head protrudes between two rafters; it would look to Rachel, if she raised her eyes, like a baby struggling to be born. "You're killing me," he shouts. She blows him a kiss with two fingers.

Comes Maria's call, he's ready for bad news. Trips getting to the phone, but he's used to his new clumsiness and snatches at the wall in time to keep himself upright.

"Listen," he tells the doctor, "I've thought of a reason. It's because I've been squatting six and eight hours a day on that slanty roof."

"No," she says. "I thought of that right away when Rachel told me what you'd been doing, but it won't do. It might make your legs sore but it wouldn't give you dropfoot."

"So what did you find out, then?"

"Nothing," she says. "You sure you didn't take a razor and cut yourself? That's a joke, Loveman. I know you didn't. Anyhow, you don't have the nervous disease. You're going to live."

"So when can I start walking again like a regular person?"

"Maybe tomorrow, maybe next week, maybe next month."

"Maybe never?"

"We mustn't give up," she tells him.

Up in the loft Rachel is silent. Building phrases in her head. Loveman sees himself as pure text. Word city. Talk about a shit sandwich. He picks up the phone again, dials.

"Maria? I've got to see you. Meet me in half an hour. I'll park across the street, we'll go to a bar. It's a matter of life and death."

He climbs the ladder to Rachel's loft, just under the unfinished roof. Above her head, the underside of his fresh shingles, heartwood, thick pages from the tree. Beyond that, blue sky sliced by rafters. Oregon sky.

"We have to have a serious talk now," Loveman says. By way of introduction he reaches under her arms to her breasts, touches the nipples. She moans and leans forward against his hands, but her fingers go on flying over the keys.

"Go away, Loveman. I'm working."

"Why don't we take a vacation," he says. "Pack up the Porsche and head for the coast, camp out, fuck under the stars, roast marshmallows?"

"No time. Got to get your book done. Don't you want to be famous?"

"It's not me you're making famous, it's my prick," Loveman says. "I wish you wouldn't do it."

"Tough titty, Loveman. Anyhow don't get to feeling too important—it's what I do with it. Without me, who'd ever know your name?"

Well it makes sense to Loveman in a weird kind of way. We all want the world to take notice. If it can't be the way we want, we'll settle for what we can get.

"But it won't really be *me*," he says.

Rachel gives that quibble the answer it deserves: silence.

"At least change the names."

Rachel shakes her head. "Not a chance. I'm into truth—it's the latest thing in fiction. Can't change anything."

"You're changing *me* all around."

"That's art," she says. "Forget it, Loveman, you'd never understand in a million years."

He checks his watch; now or never. Maria must be at the bar already, waiting for him.

"I'm going into town for a while."

"Pick up some cheese," she says. "I'll make you a surprise for dinner."

In the Porsche he discovers that he has to work the accelerator and clutch with his heels, which makes shifting gears chancy and his general progress down the road unpredictable. It's half a mile of twisty dirt down to the highway and he's lucky to make it with nothing worse than a scraped fender; once on the pavement he slips the car into high gear and lets it lug around the slow corners—if the engine suffers, it suffers. Loveman doesn't care. He heels his way into town and parks in front of a fire hydrant.

"Explain to me," Maria says. "What is life and death?"

She likes me, Loveman thinks. "I'm suffering," he says.

She taps her coffee spoon on the table. "Everybody suffers. Be specific."

"It's not my feet," he says. She's nervous, he thinks. Maybe she wants me too.

"What is it then?" she asks him. "Your life? There aren't any miracles, Loveman."

"No miracles," he says.

"You're wasting yourself," she says. "You're an intelligent person. Why aren't you doing something serious?"

"I'm building a house."

She looks at him with scorn.

"All right," Loveman says. "What should I be doing?"

"You could be anything you wanted."

"A lawyer, a teacher?" Loveman says.

"Why not?"

"A male nurse?"

"Be serious," she says. "I've met men like you before. You think you're too special to be anything."

"Let's see," Loveman says. "I could go back to school, get a degree, be an engineer. A psychologist. A social worker. An accountant, maybe."

She's laughing. "All right."

"An airline pilot," he says.

"A tailor," she says.

"A baker."

"An undertaker."

"A surveyor, a forest ranger, a farmer, a shoe salesman."

"A philosopher," she says.

"An orphan," Loveman says.

She stops laughing. "A what?"

"I love you," he says. "I've got to have you. Run away with me. We'll go anywhere you say and Rachel will never find us. Winnetka. Cincinnati. Spokane. Terre Haute. Any place you want."

"When you came to the office last week, I wanted to touch you all over," she says.

So they go. Loveman leaves the Porsche in front of the fire hydrant with a note for Rachel stuck under the windshield wiper. *Be kind to my prick. Don't be too hard on Aunt Esther either. She couldn't help what she did.* He wonders if Rachel will get the message.

2

In El Paso he and Maria rent a little house in a Mexican part of town, with a dirt yard, a saguaro cactus, and a radio that plays Spanish love songs all day long, full of flowery phrases Loveman half-understands. *La vida. Mi corazón.* Maria practices medicine in a government clinic; at night she comes home to Loveman and washes his feet with oils. It doesn't make them work any better, but it feels wonderful. He's getting used to his condition. His arms have come to be quick as lizards; they can snatch at anything handy to keep him from falling: a tree, a wall, a chair. He lurches almost gracefully from one room to another, catching himself.

During the long afternoons, while Maria practices on the poor people at the clinic, he sits in the front yard in a T-shirt, smoking cigars and getting a tan. He has grown a beard. Little kids call him *El Gringo;* when they're in a good mood they come into the yard and give him gifts of bubblegum or paper dolls. When they feel evil they throw pebbles at him from beyond the fence, but Loveman catches them with hands so quick they seem to flicker in the air. He stacks the pebbles beside his chair and when the brown devils get friendly again he hands out the rocks: two to this one, three to another, a whole handful to this little girl, who can throw better than any of them.

So it goes. Maria has stopped wanting him to make something of himself. If Loveman says he could go back to college she puts a hand over his mouth and tweaks his ear until it hurts.

"Admit it, Loveman," she says, "you love this life."

And so he does.

She brings home little tanks of nitrous oxide from the clinic, and she and Loveman suck up the stuff through rubber tubes.

"Everything is really this, but it's also really that," Loveman says under the influence. He feels himself dropping through an endless chain of opposites, cut loose from Aristotle, going down the ladder. Everything is absolutely this, and it's also absolutely that. Oh yes.

3

Rachel is out the driver's door before the Porsche stops rolling. It's a Sunday afternoon and Loveman has been watching the little kids in their go-to-church clothes parade by on the way to God knows what acts of afternoon Popery. It's all a mystery to him.

The Porsche is dusty and dented, decorated with bugs. Maria comes running out of the house and the women hug each other under the saguaro cactus. They do a little dance around each other.

"You look terrific," Rachel says. "What a cute little house. Are you pregnant or anything?"

"I'll make up a bed for you in the living room," Maria says. "How's the novel going?"

"Knopf is bringing it out in the fall," Rachel says.

"You hear that, Loveman?" Maria says.

Loveman has his eyes closed and is trying not to hear, but the voices penetrate his ears, addle his brain. Everything is absolutely this.

"And him," Rachel says. "What's happening here?"

"He's no trouble," Maria says. Loveman feels her hand on his head; she pulls his hair playfully. "Hasn't he got a beautiful tan?"

"I don't know if I like him with a beard," Rachel says. "How are the feet?"

"About the same," Maria says.

"*My* feet," Loveman says.

"Your prick too," Rachel says, "but I made it famous. The Book of the Month Club is buying it."

That night after dinner they sit in the living room and drink Mexican beer. Rachel looks lovely and Loveman wonders if she'll go to bed with him the next day, while Maria's at work.

"You could stay here as long as you want," Maria says. "There's a spare room in the back; it's a laundry room now but Loveman could fix it up with a little plaster and a new rug. You could have all the time you need to write, and he could keep you company during the day." She and Rachel smile at each other lovingly. "After all, it's not as if he could go out and get a job or anything. Not with those feet, poor baby."

Rachel brings him another beer and kisses him on the cheek. They watch over him while he drinks. Arm in arm on the green sofa they look like two sisters, one light and the other dark. He's willing to love them, he thinks, but they have to realize he's got his plans.

During the long afternoons, while Maria works at the clinic and Rachel types in the back room, he lies in the chair outside and wills his feet to get better. He finds that he can, if he concentrates totally, articulate his desire, lift the toes a fraction of a fraction of an inch. "What are you doing, man?" the little brown girl wants to know.

"Making something of myself," Loveman says. "Watch." He raises his legs; the feet still flop at the end of his ankles like two dead fish, but he concentrates and wills himself to move them.

"See that?" he says.

She shakes her head. "I don't see nothing, man."

Another little girl sneaks up behind and pinches her. She wails, runs to Loveman's lap, whispers. "Her name is Angelita." Like it was some big terrible secret.

"What's *your* name?" Loveman says.

"I don't tell you that. What you think, I'm crazy?" She hops out of his lap and tears off down the street, laughing like a loon.

Up with the toes, down with the toes, up with the toes. Loveman practices all the long afternoon. He can maybe raise them a quarter of an inch. But that's enough for now. Inside his and Maria's little house the stereo is howling love songs full of *la vida* and *mi corazón;* if he had a voice he'd sing along, but Loveman doesn't sing well and anyhow it's almost five-thirty and any minute now Maria's red Fiat should turn the end of the street.

Two women—it's a hustler's dream, but Loveman is no hustler. What he is, he doesn't know. He and Rachel tumble on the double bed in the afternoons; in the night he and Maria reinvent love. Loveman thinks she must know, but she doesn't talk about it and he's not about to open that can of worms. Not until his feet get better and he can decide what to do with his life. Often in the evenings he takes his beer out in the yard and leaves the two of them inside. The sound of their voices reaches him, but not the words. Sometimes they laugh and Loveman's hair rises on the back of his neck. He puts it down to nervousness.

Now and then Maria brings home the little tank of laughing gas and all three of them inhale like crazy, staring at each other. But Loveman has trouble letting go. Paranoid thoughts and formless fears trail him in his long tumble down the ladder of logic. He worries about what's at the bottom. If everything is absolutely this and also absolutely the opposite, what's left?

Maria takes the tube out of her mouth and speaks. What she says Loveman doesn't hear, because it takes her too long. In the space between the two words Loveman works out three complete systems of metaphysics, each a little more comprehensive than the last. He hears the words, but by the time one arrives he's forgotten the one that came before.

Rachel speaks. Then Maria.

Then Loveman, but he has to hurry because otherwise the two sisters will get bored waiting for his next word and he won't get across this very important message. Which he knows full well is of no importance whatever. And also is as vital as anything they're likely to hear in this life. But how important is that, after all? Down the ladder, hugging *claritas* and *quidditas* to his chest. If everything is absolutely that, and also absolutely this, what's left? Everything.

Words that come one at a time, without the possibility of context. Loveman feels them falling through his ears like little blank stones. Rachel speaks. Maria speaks. She says. They say. One-note tunes.

"*La vida,*" Loveman says. "*Mi corazón.*"

He can walk. He gets up out of his chair and dances across the room, flexing the toes, arching the feet. Tippy-toes to the couch where the two women are sitting arm in arm, does a little soft-shoe, a buck-and-wing, a Texas two-step.

"Look," he says. "Look at me now."

Later he wakes up alone in the double bed; low voices in the living room sound urgent, but not as urgent as his thoughts. He thinks back about the dream, throws the covers to one side because he can't stand not to know for sure and dreams are foolers. He tries his toes. They move. No dream. He could walk like a normal person. Too sleepy to try it now, he promises himself joy in the morning. He'll leap and prance and astonish Maria and Rachel. Won't they be pleased!

He wakes up one more time, smelling the hot sweet El Paso air coming through the bedroom window. Two shadows are sitting on the foot of the bed. Maria is searching through the black medical bag she always carries with her; her hand comes out holding a scalpel that catches a beam of moonlight and gleams wickedly. Loveman tries to move but Rachel is sitting across his legs.

"It'll only take a second," Maria says. "He'll hardly feel it at all."

Cheerful Wisdom

"**L**isten now, honey. I am about to tell you the God's simple truth about all this, from the start to the finish. No lies."

My wife watches me across the kitchen table with sleepy eyes. She has hair rich as cream. Skin like a baby's behind, for all that she's my age. A miracle, I mean. Titties I'd die for. But right this second I tell myself: *don't touch*. It's about six in the morning, I suppose; I left my watch someplace. The kitchen looks about the same as it did three days ago, only worse: dishes smeared with fossil food are piled in the sink like leaning towers. Crusty pots and pans on the stove. It looks trashy, but then I am not in such good shape myself that I have a right to complain. My breath smells and my armpits are rancid. My face is stubbly and I have dog shit on one shoe from not watching my step when I came across the lawn. The smell is awful. The situation is precarious. I'd like some coffee but I'm not about to ask.

"Three days," she says. "What have you been doing? Where have you been?"

We have known each other since high school, but are only lately married. The years look better on her than they do on me: plumped-out, ripe. She works down at the Tyler General Hospital; the patients quiver when she comes tappity-tap down the hall in her high-heeled nurse's shoes; the doctors all get hard-ons. So she tells me. She is a tough lady with a mind that I have learned to respect. Reads Camus. Swallows insights into the human condition like some people pop pills. She knows more than I do about life.

"Never mind for a minute," I tell her. "It's bad news anyway."

We went through high school together like a second-rate American dream. She was an alternate cheerleader and I sat on the bench during the football season. I took my lumps in practice and she went through her routines in front of the mirror in her parents' living room. We should have learned patience, but we didn't.

"It starts with the Chinaman," I say. "But it doesn't end there."

"What bad news?" she says.

That's how she is—always wanting to go to the heart of the matter. I like to take my time, circle a little, get ready. The heart'll still be there when I want it.

"I don't suppose I have ever told you about the Chinaman. Every time I go up to the field house to play racquetball with your Uncle Ezra I see him up there in the locker room lying on a wooden bench, stark naked except for a little white cloth covering his organs."

"Hrrm," she says. She yawns. Thus encouraged I continue.

"With his eyes closed. He's a sight. If I could draw I would draw him for you. He has the real Confucius beard, which is long and pointy. Few hairs, relatively speaking, but long ones. His eyes are always closed. Thinking enormous thoughts, but calm."

"Did it ever occur to you he was just asleep?" says my wife.

"If he wanted to sleep he could sleep anywhere," I tell her. "In any case this isn't a story about the China-man, but about your Uncle Ezra, who we will get to in a minute. The Chinaman is just the cause of what happened. I wish you could have seen him. A splendid face. He has the sort of wrinkles that come from knowing things, not the kind of lines you get from just being beaten around by life. Wisdom, I'm trying to say. That's what I told Ezra."

"Hrrm," she says.

Call that talking? I could be dying right here across the table from her, of a busted heart, like poor Ezra. Would she care?

"What's the bad news?" she says.

"Wait. You know I've always thought a lot about those Eastern religions. I've read Alan Watts, I've read Ginsberg, I've studied Kerouac. Life is an illusion. And now here's this Chinaman I've been seeing three days a week for the past four years. He lies absolutely still. A perfect body which, besides being the same gorgeous yellow all over, has no body hair, no pores. Like he was carved out of one piece of old ivory."

"Everybody has pores."

"I looked close and couldn't see a sign of one," I say. "Nobody pays any attention to him lying there. It's always quiet in that part of the locker room where he is. Nobody snapping towels at each other's butts or hollering 'I want pussy!' or throwing the soap around. All he needs to be is *there*, for it to be silent. I can tell he's got no desires, no wants. No little voice like we all have, that says *I need, I want, I have to have, I deserve*."

"You have a little voice like that?" my wife says.

"You do too. Don't give me any shit. I know we're the same."

"Hrrm," she says. It's an all-purpose noise. The light

is getting stronger through the window. Rosy-fingered
dawn. I might only be an optometrist but I know a
thing or two myself. I've read the classics.

"Don't be so goddamned certain," she says. That we
are alike, I think she means. All she has on her body,
because I got her up out of bed to let me in, having
also lost my house keys along with my watch, is a little
shortie robe of some red silky stuff. One titty is peering
out and I'd give up a finger to touch it, even in my
present exhausted condition. I can see her thighs,
which are the color of wholewheat bread because at the
hospital she sneaks into the linen closet with a sunlamp
and strips off her clothes. God help me but I love this
woman. So why are things not working out? I blame
myself.

"My big mistake was getting into this whole racquetball thing with your uncle," I tell her. "Just because
he's rich."

Ezra is like a man-size yellow dog. A whiner. Veins
breaking out all over him like a spring thaw. An old
man in very poor shape, but an excellent racquetball
player. He has a backhand lob serve that skins the wall
and dies in the corner while I beat my head into the
floor trying to make a retrieve. The mangy old bastard
can put spins on the ball that make it sit up and beg
while I fall over my two feet trying to swap directions.
He wins, I lose. I lose, he wins. But afterwards in the
shower what a hairy limp-dicked awfulness he is. Folds
of fat come out of Ezra's head and ripple down him
like an obscene meat-fountain. The college boys can't
take their eyes off him; they don't believe the human
body could come to this.

"Admit it," my wife says. "You just don't like being
beaten by an older man."

"It would be all right if he didn't apologize after-
ward. That's the part I hate."

She wrinkles her nose. "This kitchen smells like dog shit," she says. "What have you been doing? Where have you been?"

"We're coming to that."

"We'd better," she says.

"But first I want to ask you something. Did Ezra ever try to feel you up or anything when you were little?"

She looks down. "Just regular uncle stuff," she says.

"Such as what?"

"He used to grab my parts and yell cheerful things."

"Your what?"

"Parts," she says. She blushes. "You know."

Do I ever. I'm dying to grab them myself right now. But this isn't the moment. Patience, I tell myself.

"You never yell cheerful things when *you* touch me," she says. "All you ever do is moan."

"What kinds of things would you like me to yell?" I ask her.

"Use your imagination."

I reach out under the table. "Apple pie!" I shout. She grabs my wrist and presses my hand to the place. I can't help it: I moan.

She pushes me away and slaps my hand viciously. "There," she says. "You see?"

"It's unnatural not to expect me do that."

"Go on with your story," she says. "Not that I believe it."

"It's the God's truth," I say. "Monday last, which was three days ago, I finished my game with Ezra and he said he was sorry to beat me so bad again. 'You've got good strokes,' he said. 'I admire the hell out of the way you swing that racket. Haar, haar, it looks terrific.' "

"He has always been generous with his praise," my wife says.

"God knows I forgive him now," I say. "But he was a man made out of mud. A walking slump-pile. An appetite with legs and arms to carry it around. All the time he was telling me what great strokes I made, he had his yellow teeth sunk in his racket handle, sucking and chewing like an orphan."

"He's a wealthy man," she says.

"I've got a respectable trade. I don't have to take any shit from Ezra because he's got millions."

"You've got a one-man office in the shopping mall," she reminds me nastily.

"I do all right."

"You're a nothing man," she says. "I don't know why I like you. In fact I'm not certain I do."

"What else did Uncle Ezra do besides grab you and shout cheerful things?" I ask her.

"Once he came to my bedroom and licked me like a dog," she admits.

"Why the old bastard," I say with admiration. "I never thought he had it in him. I thought he was just ugly and somebody left him money in their will."

"Never mind Uncle Ezra," says my wife. "I want an explanation of where you have been."

Suddenly it seems to me that I'm embarked on a dubious and desperate enterprise here. Old rosy-fingers is blasting through the kitchen window, lighting up the pots and pans and the pyramid of dishes in the sink; the birds are firing up out there in front of the house, working out the kinks and getting ready to holler; up the street, front doors are slamming and my neighbors are coming out in bathrobes, scratching their asses, and sticking their heads under the oleander bushes to see where the morning paper is. And I'm sitting here having solemnly promised to tell the absolute truth. Lordy-be-to-Jesus. Sleepy-eyes is waiting for me to get on with it, and there's nothing in my head but lies I have sworn I wouldn't tell.

"Let me touch you." I'm begging. "I promise not to moan. Let me."

"Fat chance," says she. "Get on with your story."

"All right," I say. "But brace yourself because here comes the bad news now. Look out and be ready. The Chinaman was the cause of it all. When I came out to the front lobby to turn in my locker key, there he was, not only fully dressed like an ordinary human being, but wearing a three-piece suit. My man of wisdom that I had been telling Ezra about. Dressed in a snazzy black pinstripe with a cream-colored silk shirt and Countess Mara tie. Uncle Ezra, the second he sees this vision, starts whooping and hollering and coughing. 'Wisdom,' he says. 'Wisdom! Haar, haar, haar!'

"The Chinaman turns around to see who or what is making all this wheezy commotion. Uncle Ezra is trying to get a cigar out of his shirt pocket; with the free hand he is digging into his trousers for change for the candy machine. The snorts and wheezes and chortles are rolling out of him and he's shaking all over and can't catch his breath. In a minute he's begun to turn an unhealthy shade of purple and his eyes are popping out of his head. I've never seen him so happy.

"The Chinaman nods. 'I know you,' says he. 'Whoo!' says Ezra. He staggers back into the wall and knocks down a poster that says *Accept Jesus Christ as Your Personal Savior.* The Chinaman advances until he and your uncle are nearly nose to nose. By all appearances Ezra is about one half-second from going up the flume with an exploded heart; his face is the color of an eggplant, his breath is irregular, he's having the time of his life. 'You and your man of wisdom,' he says to me. 'Oriental religions. Life is illusion. He looks like a stockbroker, haar, haar, haar.'

"The Chinaman is looking at him; he's never seen

anything just like this before. Ezra is beginning to slide down the wall, still laughing. 'Buy low, sell high,' he says between snorts and wheezes."

"What did you do?" my wife says.

"What could I do? People were looking. A crowd. Death draws them in."

"He's a fine man," my wife says. "He may have fondled me when I was little, but he didn't mean anything by it. I'm his only living relative. It was just uncle stuff. He couldn't be dead."

"It happened like this," I tell her. "Uncle Ezra's eyes went rolling back in his head; one hand came jerking out of his pants pocket and quarters, dimes, nickels, and half-dollars went dancing and jingling all over the lobby floor under people's feet; his other hand was holding a broken White Owl cigar which he was waving in the Chinaman's face."

"Oh God," my wife says.

"Ezra was sitting down, still trying to stick the cigar in his mouth. 'Speak softly and carry a big stick.' he said, and began to chew on the cigar. When I bent over him he was dead."

"Dead?" my wife says.

"Like a shotgunned rabbit," I tell her gently. "I forgive him all the evil things he did to you. Anyhow, they were a long time ago."

"And where have you been?" she says, returning to the original question.

"His heart popped like a paper bag, dearest. It's no use to mourn; he died the way he lived: carnally. An evil old dog, but I don't hold a grudge."

"I might hold one against you," she says. "What have you been doing since Monday?"

"Maybe it's better not to ask," I tell her. "Let bygones be bygones. Would it really matter if I'd been so upset about this that I had gone on a three-day bender and screwed every available woman in town? If I had got drunk and disorderly and took my pants down in front of the old ladies in the park? As a way of showing grief?"

"For Uncle Ezra?"

"It's more complicated than that. I wouldn't lie to you. He was a mangy old dog."

"You're something of a dog yourself," she says, thinking it over.

"Don't shoot till you see the whites of their eyes," I tell her, trying to show that I learned something from Ezra at the end.

"Touch me now," she says.

"Blue Moon!" is what I shout in her ear.

We fall out of our chairs and thrash around indecently on the kitchen linoleum covered with tiny blue flowers. Never mind the dog shit; we're going to be millionaires. It's our lovely second-rate life I'm mourning for. Who would have thought, when she was doing routines in her living room and I sat on the bench, that we'd end up like this? It's very sad. I pull up her robe and begin to lick her like a dog. We have obligations. I can feel that in a minute I'm going to start sucking and chewing. It's the human condition.

Sometimes the Wrong Thing Is the Right Thing

The other six nights at the Joker belong to the semiprofessional eighteen-year-olds with too much breast, too little hip, and all the assurance in the world, flashy girls with hard little asses no bigger than volleyballs, who strut their stuff, roll their eyes at the men, and end up being about as sexy as Shirley Temple. But on Saturday, starting at seven and going on as long as the supply of volunteers holds out, it's these other women. They are generally older, in their late twenties or even thirties, and they have real bodies. Bodies that have seen more of life than the local motel or the back seats of cars, or the little room at home with the teddy bears on the wallpaper. When they come on stage and begin to sway to the music of the Troubadours, to unzip and unsnap and unbutton, things change. Watch the men who watch these older women and you can see that the fantasies are different. Darker. Serious ideas are being worked out under the Resistol hats then. Listen to the big men breathe, look at the eyes. All the lightheartedness that comes with the eighteen-year-olds is gone now.

"What are we doing here, Linda-Sue?" Charlie asks me.

It's Saturday, amateur night, and fifteen or twenty

women are waiting backstage for their turn to step out under the purple spotlights and take their clothes off while Floyd Thatcher and his boys play good serious country music. One of the fifteen or twenty is my sister Stella, Charlie's wife.

"We're here to carry on with your sentimental education," I tell Charlie.

He stubs out his seventeenth Marlboro Light and looks at me patiently. Stella has taught him patience. Before he married her he didn't know much about life, but he could look you in the eye clear and certain. Now more and more every day he has a funny expression, as if one of his friends at Al's Body Shop had tapped him behind the ear with the big rubber-headed hammer they use to pound out dents. Dazed, I mean, though I am sorry to say I see hope there too.

"What's that supposed to mean?" Charlie says. "Sentimental education?"

"Oh, Charlie, haven't you ever read a book?"

"I read one every week," he says. He does, but they are serious books, not fiction, which he calls lies. He taps a Marlboro out of the pack and hands it across the table. I take it because I know I just made him feel bad. Lots of people walk through life wearing a sign that says Kick Me, but that doesn't mean you have to. Charlie wants desperately to be a *good* person, and my sister Stella is helping him as hard as she can. She seems to believe being hurt is the best way to learn to be good.

I am nervous and as far as I can tell by looking across the table at him Charlie is dazed, puzzled, hopeful. Maybe more than a little sad too. I think he suspects that he and Stella are coming to the end of the road, and there is not much in his life to replace being married, unless you count playing stud poker Friday nights with his buddies from the body shop, and once a year taking a week off to go fly-fishing by himself on a little river in Idaho.

"After all, she's my sister," I say, as much to myself as to Charlie. "My own flesh and blood."

"Don't worry. She'll be the best," he says.

"And it doesn't make you feel peculiar at all?"

"Why would it?" he says.

It is in Stella's mind that Charlie will learn something by watching his wife prance naked in front of strangers. Actually not strangers—I could look around this crowded, smoky room and name half the people. Better if it *was* strangers, instead of Perry Hoffer and the Thibodeaux brothers and half a dozen more who will spread the story all over town by tomorrow. Maybe he *will* learn something by it—Charlie is no dummy—but I don't think that what he learns will do him any good in life. I went out with Charlie for a while, just after we all graduated from high school—he has a wonderful body, all wires and ropes that slide under his skin and are wonderful to touch—but there was not what you would call love between us, and so I gave him up. I have always kept on liking Charlie, but in some way I don't completely understand, it pleases me to see Stella teach him every day that life is not as simple as he thought it was. My sister is a real professor of sentiment and she's got Charlie enrolled in the advanced course.

"Does it bother *you?*" Charlie says.

"She's only my sister but she's your wife. She's about to get up there and get naked in a minute. You mean to say it's all right with you?"

"Naked is just a word," Charlie says. His eyes are smarting a little from all the smoke, but he won't weep. "Men are the same as women," he says. "If I wanted to stand up there and take my clothes off in front of

everybody I could, couldn't I? Nobody would think it
was wrong. So why not Stella? Though I don't want to
do it, but that isn't the point."

"Is that one of her speeches?" I ask him. "Did she
make you learn it by heart?" I smile so he'll know I
didn't mean it to make him feel bad.

The girl who is on stage now was in my geometry
class in high school. She is having herself a good time.
Her husband was killed last year off one of the oil
platforms, and she has been waiting until she gets
through the insurance money before she finds herself
another man. She is already down to her bra and
panties, and people around us are perking up. Even
Charlie has changed the angle of his slouch so he can
see. Not that she is a beauty, but there is something in
her face, some wacky combination of innocence and
lust that tickles our hearts.

Charlie and I have been here for amateur night before, but it was always with Stella holding Charlie's
hand and explaining to him why each of those women
was up there taking off her clothes. Why it was necessary. Tonight because she is backstage waiting her turn
everything is different. Instead of watching Charlie
swallow her arguments and feeling sorry for him, I am
remembering what it was like when he and I went out
together, before I decided there wasn't love between
us. I am feeling things about Charlie that I haven't felt
in years. Itchy things.

"Men are the same as women," Charlie says again.

I take his hand and squeeze it. The girl who used to
be in my class is teasing us, reaching around her back
to unsnap her little filmy bra, spinning under the lights
while Floyd Thatcher plays "Yesterday's Wine" as slow
and sexy as he can.

Another boyfriend once told me that if he could

come back after death as anything at all he wanted to
be born again as a pedal steel—all that twangy wonder-
fulness, all those slow-to-die notes. He's a poet now
someplace in Alabama; every now and then he sends
me one of his poems, full of down-home phrases and
steely sentiments.

Charlie looks down at where our hands are lying
together on the table, and frowns. "The human body
isn't anything to be ashamed of," he says. "Famous
people have their pictures naked in magazines all the
time."

I'd like to kiss him. Instead I say, "Burt Reynolds."

"Marilyn Monroe on that calendar," he says. "Nobody thinks worse of her because of that picture, do
they?"

Two tables down from where we sit Perry Hoffer,
who runs the cafe next door to Al's Body Shop, is
grinning stupidly into his beer; at the table behind him
the Thibodeaux brothers are stamping their feet more
or less in time to the music. They played left tackle and
right tackle, or maybe the other way around, on our
high school team; now they sell insurance and have
snappy blonde wives who are not with them at the
Joker tonight.

"I don't think it's a question of the human body,
Charlie. We're talking about something different
here."

He removes his hand from mine so he can light himself one more cigarette. "You never really liked Stella,"
he announces.

What right has he got to say that? "She's my sister," I
tell him. "Naturally I like her."

"Sisters often don't like each other," he goes on, as if
I had never said anything.

We sit and stare at each other for a while like two

dogs ready to kiss or fight and not knowing which they'd rather. He's brown-eyed and tall, a handsome man, and he's more intelligent than most of the men I've known in my life. Why is he doing this? If I asked him he'd say for love, if he even knew what I meant.

His cigarette is almost down to the filter but he doesn't know it; his right hand is clenched around his beer and the left hand is beating hard time on the table. My old acquaintance has her bra off and is twirling it by the strap. I can hear the men breathing; one of the Thibodeaux brothers whistles softly. It's not the same noise the men make when the eighteen-year-olds are up there bouncing too much breast and bumping their hips. This woman has small breasts like mine, like Stella's, hard as green apples. They lift when she twirls the bra around her head, teasing the boys. Her eyes are innocent, as if she is saying to all these men, "What do you think you're looking at that's so interesting?" Floyd works a bunch of low, fine-sounding notes out of the pedal steel and she understands what he means and hooks a finger under the elastic of her panties, looking out at us all the while through the smoke.

"Do you think she's intelligent?" Charlie says.

"You mean Stella? I suppose so."

"She was never any good in school, but that was because she didn't want to be."

"She has never thought of herself as an ordinary person," I tell him.

He's looking at me. His face is serious. His left hand is still beating time on the tabletop. "True intelligence is *doing* things," he says. "Not just reading books and talking smart. It's *being*," he says.

Even when we were in high school Charlie was a serious one. The other boys thought about making the team and getting into as many girls' pants as they could; Charlie didn't care for sports, though he was strong and quick. He read books about how to homestead your own land in Alaska or how to make a fortune in real estate with only a hundred dollars to start. What *I* read was foolishness to him. "You say it's fiction, but it's only lies," he would tell me while he unbuttoned my sweater in the back seat of his father's Buick Roadmaster. "Where is there any truth in it?" It was one of the reasons there wasn't love between us after all.

"It's doing what you know to be the right thing," he says now. Somewhere back there out of sight my sister is getting ready to do things; before we left the house I asked her if it was necessary for Charlie and me to be there to watch her. She dug her fingers into my shoulder until it hurt, and squinted her eyes like Clint Eastwood. "You bet," she told me.

The place is overcrowded like it always is on Saturday night, full of fat men trying to be cowboys; they are loaded down with silver and turquoise and squeezed into tight pants until it's God's own miracle they can breathe.

I reach over and take Charlie by the hand. "Why don't you let me drive you back to the house," I tell him. "Stella thinks she needs to do this, but there is no reason you ought to have to see it. You and I can have a couple of beers and look at the TV and wait for her to come home."

He hasn't gained a pound since high school; the ropes and wires are still right there under the skin where I could touch them. I think suddenly that maybe the best thing I could do for Charlie is put him in my bed and take that puzzled look out of his eyes for a little while. Maybe it's all the emotion in here that gives me an idea like that, all the breathing we can hear even above the band, a big sad wind blowing up before a storm. It would be wrong for me and Charlie to go to bed together, but not as wrong as it is for the two of us to sit here waiting to see Stella climb up on the stage and teach Charlie one more thing he doesn't need to know. Sometimes one wrong thing is better than another.

"Charlie."

"Hush," he says. "It's her turn now."

Stella is a year younger than I am, and Charlie is wrong—I have always liked her. But I have always known that she was truly different from everybody else, though maybe until tonight I haven't been ready to say that I knew it. She isn't crazy, exactly, but she doesn't live in the same world as Charlie and me or the Thibodeaux brothers or the fat men and their girlfriends breathing heavy at the next table. In the world where Stella lives, there is nobody but her. I mean if you asked point-blank she would look you in the eye and say, "Of course there are other people out there." But I think that deep down where it counts she can't quite make herself believe it. Maybe this is why she acts like she does, so somebody will get angry enough at her to prove they are there too, and then she won't be so lonely any more.

"Charlie," I whisper. I want to take him home right now. It's not too late. Perry Hoffer is talking low to his girlfriend; the Thibodeaux brothers are yawning and scratching themselves, waiting for the show to go on. It's dead wrong for them to see Charlie seeing this.

"Charlie."

"Hush now," he says. His hand is shaking a little but his face is solemn.

Stella is wearing the dress she bought last Christmas when she made Charlie take her to the Country Club dance. It is faded rose satin, high-necked, trimmed with lace. Under the purple lights the faded rose shines purely white, and it looks to everybody like she is standing there in her wedding dress. Even the Troubadours are a little startled by her appearance, and she stands there for five or ten seconds, stock-still under the spotlights, before Floyd Thatcher pulls himself together and starts the music. Even now, I tell myself, if she has picked the right song it might all be a joke. But when the Troubadours start to play "Good-hearted Woman" I see that Stella is as solemn as Charlie, and if it is a joke it is not the kind of joke that any person with a good heart could laugh at.

"Did you ever see her so beautiful?" Charlie says.

I tell him no. My heart is breaking and at the same time I am feeling so itchy for a touch of Charlie that I can't stand it. I can feel my breaking heart pumping blood out to the ends of my body, stirring up little veins, blowing up the tips of my fingers like balloons. I can hardly believe it when I look down at the table and see my fingers look the same as always. Charlie is watching his wife through half-closed eyes; Stella undoes the front of her dress button by button, swaying softly to the music. Behind us the Thibodeaux brothers are whispering to each other.

"You'd have to *know* her," Charlie says.

I'd like him to touch me, but he's lost in Stella, watching her every move.

"It's wrong," I tell him.

"No it's not," he says.

"Why not?"

"Because she's special," he says. "More special than you, even if you don't think so." He puts a cheating spin on the words, so that they take off and fly into the smoke with a power all their own to make things different. I want to tell him one or two truths of my own, about what's right and wrong, about the Thibodeaux brothers and Perry Hoffer and even Floyd Thatcher who sits up there behind his pedal steel looking innocent and proud of himself. But I keep my mouth shut and my eyes on Stella. The pink satin dress is open all the way down the front and she's shrugging her way out of it. She's not a good dancer, but I can tell it's not important: this is not a dance, exactly.

"Get naked, sweetheart," Charlie says. I look at his face and it hasn't changed. Hopeful, puzzled, expecting God knows what kind of wisdom to come from this experience.

I have seen Stella naked more times than I can remember, so I know it's not the sight of her breasts, so much like mine, that is making me feel itchy and stirred up inside. Anyhow women's bodies don't do anything for me in that way. They are too soft, too smooth, not like Charlie's with all those steely wires. So what it is that's making me hot and tingly I don't know.

"Charlie," I say, "why did you and Stella get married?"

"Love," he says, as if it was the most natural thing in the world. He's not looking at me. The Thibodeaux brothers are leaning forward with their Resistol hats tilted up on their foreheads and their eyes popping. Perry Hoffer is feverishly kneading his girlfriend's thigh under her dress. Somebody whispers, "Do it, honey! For God's sake do it!" like the prayer that it is. We have a moment of passionate intensity while Stella slips out of her bra one shy breast at a time; her mouth is slightly open, showing her good teeth. The big men are grunting and wheezing. Charlie looks proud.

"What do you know about love?" I ask him.

"What's anybody *know* about it?" he says. "It's something you feel, not something you study up."

Charlie always believed in the emotions. Leave it to him, he'd let a feeling stir and stew about inside himself for five or six years before he'd be sure it was the real thing and trot it out. "Talking about things is lying about them" is another proposition he explained to me in the back seat of the Roadmaster. I was looking up from underneath, past his head, at a full moon and the tops of the scrub oaks, and when he said that I wanted to cry because I knew I could do nothing else except give him up for good.

"Do you love her now, Charlie?" I ask him.

I can see the dimple where she broke her collarbone falling off a horse in the tenth grade and it never healed quite right, and the little half-moon scar on her thigh where she stabbed herself with Daddy's fishing knife. The dress that Charlie bought her is lying in a heap next to the drummer, her bra and panties are draped across the front of the stage, and the white satin pumps she wore to the Country Club dance are laid neatly side by side pointing away from us, the way you would put them under the bed last thing at night before settling down with your husband.

It's supposed to be the end of the act. The Troubadours are getting ready to give it a couple of final licks. Stella will glide out from under the spotlights with one last *haven't we had a good time, fellers* smile for the customers.

Only I can see she's not ready to call it quits. She stands where she is, with her arms raised over her head, waiting. Floyd stares at her, puzzled, then finally shrugs and strums the pedal steel one more time. "Good-hearted Woman." My sister starts into that slow

dance which is not a dance but something more serious, her arms lifted up to heaven, her legs spread
apart a little, her hips twisting in time with the music,
but not *moved* by it, as if Floyd and the Troubadours
could stop any time and it wouldn't matter a bit,
though as long as they're playing anyhow she'll do
them the politeness to pretend it's the pedal steel moving her, instead of something that has nothing to do
with anybody else at all.

"Charlie," I say. But he's gone from me into that
other place where nobody but Stella is allowed to be. I
could have loved him if he had believed in lies, like I
do, like everybody who has any sense, the lies which
are the only things that can save us.